Love, Anon

Bryony Rosehurst

Copyright © 2021 Bryony Rosehurst

Content Warnings

Mentions of alcohol addiction and toxic relationships

One

@BlushinginBrooklyn: Have been secretly and catastrophically in love with my yoga instructor for the last three years. I don't even like yoga, but I force myself to go every week for her. Anyway, today I passed gas while in Downward Dog — and she was standing directly behind me as it happened. Will never be able to show my face in her studio again. What a tragic conclusion to our unrequited love story.

Quinn laughed into her Absinthe Frappé — a dangerous choice of cocktail for brunch — as she read aloud from the app on her phone. The screen's silver light illuminated her pale face and the fact that it was still streaked with last night's mascara.

"Please don't talk about breaking wind in a fancy cafe." Arden pursed her lips in disapproval, tracing a light, paint-speckled finger around the rim of her cappuccino. Her eyes darted back to the corner of the cafe where the door to the restrooms lay between the old red brickwork and chalkboard menus. It was the third time she had done this in minutes. What the hell was taking their dad so long? He knew better than to leave Arden alone with her sister. She'd been biting down on a lecture all morning after Quinn had rocked up in a sparkly, high-hemmed dress, claiming that she hadn't had time to change when she'd gotten in from partying *this morning*.

Arden loved her sister dearly, but she was tired of watching her morph into their mom. When the parties turned sour and Quinn's no-good boyfriends found other women to cling on to instead, Arden would always be the one to pick up the pieces. It was exhausting, watching history repeat itself. Exhausting and gut-wrenching.

Quinn rolled her eyes. "Okay, *Mom*."

If Arden were their mom, she'd have been crashing on a friend's couch or disappearing on a four-night bender instead of paying for her sister's brunch, but she did her best to let the insult slide past her. She rolled her shoulders back in an attempt to ease up.

"What app is it, anyway? Twitter?" In an attempt at feigning interest, Arden braced her elbows on the round table and picked at her avocado toast. Quinn had already devoured her chocolate-drenched waffle, the same one she'd ordered every weekend for the past fifteen years — a tradition that their dad had started just to get them out of the house on a Sunday morning when their mom was hungover. Despite being Arden's older sister, Quinn had stopped maturing somewhere around her seventeenth year. In turn,

Arden had become the uncool and sensible nagging one when it should have been the other way around.

"No, it's some anonymous dating thing," Quinn replied, sighing and locking her phone. She swiped her finger across her plate of devoured food, licking away the last remnants of syrup. "Random strangers post about their love lives, but you can also use it to find blind dates if you want, or just to vent about your day. You should try it out, actually."

Arden raised an eyebrow, watching absently as a man outside struggled to kick the kickstand up from his chained bike. "I'm good, thanks. Sounds like a magnet for creeps and perverts."

"Who's a creepy pervert?" Finally, their dad returned to the table, still tucking the tail of his shirt into his tailored trousers. As he sat down, the perfumed scent of the restaurant's fancy French hand soap wafted over them. The scent of rich, creamy coffee followed as a waiter placed down another latte for their dad and a cappuccino for Arden. Thank God he hadn't gotten Quinn a refill.

"Quinn," Arden said at the same time Quinn replied, "We were just talking about Don't Be a Stranger. It's a fun new dating app."

"Dating app? I thought you were still with whatshisface?" Their dad's grey eyebrows knitted together, and he gestured wildly as though it would clarify who he meant.

Arden's features tautened with a bitterness

she had long since stopped trying to hide. *Whatshisface* was Leo, and he was a first-class prick who treated Quinn like trash. No matter how many times Arden pointed out as much, usually after they'd had an argument or Arden had tolerated him at a family dinner, Quinn always went back to him.

Quinn shrugged. "Well, yeah, I am, but it's not just a dating app. You can post whatever you feel like. And his name is Leo, by the way. You've met him, like, three times."

"And will you be bringing *Leo* to Christmas dinner this year?" their dad asked pointedly. He approved of Quinn's long line of shitty boyfriends about as much as Arden did, but he also preached that they were *her* mistakes to make. Arden had a feeling that their dad didn't know just *how* many mistakes Quinn was making on a daily basis these days.

"Maybe. I'll ask."

"What about you, Ard?" Their dad's icy eyes fell to Arden, and Arden tried to stifle a shudder against the weight of them. "Seeing anyone?"

Arden feigned nonchalance, batting him away with her hand and mumbling something not even she could decipher.

"You *are* dating again, aren't you?"

Her breath hitched at the question, then she lifted her gaze from the froth of her coffee to find her father's features lined with disarming, piercing concern. She was so tired of seeing it.

So tired of everybody looking at her like she was broken.

"It's been over a year, sweetheart…" her dad continued, worrying at his bottom lip. "I really think you should put yourself out there ag—"

"I am. I'm dating someone." The words — the *lie* — fell from her lips without warning. Arden couldn't take another lecture or another dose of pity. She couldn't take everybody telling her what she should be doing, how she should be moving on. Her marriage had ended. She was divorced. It was treated as a tragic label, as though she'd died a pathetic death the day she'd signed the papers. Though Arden was content with her independence, her family still didn't seem to be.

Her dad brightened, a toothy grin spreading across his chiselled face. "That's great news! Bring them along to dinner next week. I want to meet them."

"Oh, I don't know —"

But her dad wasn't listening. As he was rising from his chair, pulling on his jacket, and checking his watch, Arden's chance to take back her words was quickly dwindling.

"Gotta dash, girls. I said I'd meet Murray and his parents at Grand Central. They're coming to stay for the weekend, heaven help me." Murray was their dad's new husband. Though Arden got along with her step-father well, his parents were dreary at best…

Their dad planted a kiss on each of their

cheeks, made rough by the beginnings of salt-and-pepper stubble. "I'll see you and your guests next week?"

Arden sighed defeatedly and waved him away. "See you next week."

"Bye," Quinn called, already back to scrolling on her phone.

As soon as the glass door swung shut behind his retreating figure, Arden slumped into her plate of avocado toast, the cutlery clattering against her pointy elbows.

"You're not dating anybody, are you?" Quinn questioned knowingly.

"No." For all the splinters in their relationship, Arden had never been any good at lying to Quinn. So she didn't try now. "I just wanted him to get off my back. He looks at me like…" She cringed, remembering the sympathy swimming in their dad's eyes. "Like I'm damaged goods. Like I'm pathetic."

"You *are* a little pathetic." Quinn's voice was light, teasing, but Arden still shot her daggers. "Oh, come on. It's fine. We can find you a date for the day, and then he'll stop pestering you and you can go back to being a lonely old spinster."

"I'm not lonely," Arden snapped, and it wasn't a complete lie. Maybe there was the occasional dark winter night spent curled up, crying into her hot chocolate while watching predictable Hallmark rom-coms, but most of the time… she was fine. Her marriage had been over

6

for a long time, well before the divorce had been settled, and she didn't particularly miss having somebody to answer to every night because she'd been working too hard in the pottery studio to notice how late it was or to pick up her phone. She could do what she wanted now, with no obligation to explain herself to anyone. That freedom wasn't something she'd be willing to give up again so soon.

Quinn hummed distractedly, typing something into her phone. "I have an idea. Wanted…" she murmured in time to the clicks of her chipped nails. "Temporary Christmas date. Must be cute, no older than forty, and willing to pretend to be in a relationship for the sake of a nosy, judgemental dad —"

"What are you doing?" Panic lanced through Arden as she snatched Quinn's battered phone away. The words were midway through being typed out on a white screen. In the corner, the purple heart-shaped logo for Don't Be a Stranger winked at her.

Before Arden could delete the message, Quinn tugged the phone back and squirmed in her chair so that Arden couldn't seize it again. "Payment: homemade Christmas dinner. Must come equipped with pumpkin pie and vodka. Any and all genders welcome… Rainbow emoji."

"*Quinn!*" Arden shot up and reached for the phone, but it was too late. The *swoosh* of the submit button sounded through the din of clattering coffee cups and squealing chair legs. "No... You didn't."

"Yes, I did." A triumphant grin broke like winter sunlight across Quinn's lipstick-stained mouth. "Come on, Arden. It'll make Dad happy. Plus, Savannah said she's had some good hookups from this app. Maybe you'll get more than just pie." She wiggled her brows suggestively.

Arden's cheeks burned. She slowly lowered to her chair, glowering at her sister. "I hate you."

"I know," Quinn chirped, slipping her phone into her purse. "I'll let you know if I get any responses. Anyway, I need to sleep off this absinthe. Good night." She blew Arden a kiss and hooked her purse across her shoulder, leaving Arden alone at a table of empty glasses and dirty plates.

Arden huffed out a frustrated breath, crossed her legs, and gulped down the rest of her coffee. She winced. It had gone cold.

Logically, she knew she could back out of whatever mess Quinn had just started. She didn't *have* to invite a perfect stranger to dinner so that she could pretend she was dating again. She could turn up alone and spend the holidays swathed in sympathetic glances and not so subtle suggestions of her sad, lonely existence. Or she could claim that the person she was dating was busy and couldn't make it, but... her family probably wouldn't buy it. At least she wouldn't feel like a complete loser if Quinn *did* find her a date. Then again, a fake one might have been even sadder than going alone.

Arden swallowed down a curse. She couldn't do this. She *wouldn't* do this.

Would she?

Two

@LookingforLove: *Dear potter on E 12th Street,*

I pass your studio each day on my commute to work and always, without fail, am reminded of that one scene in Ghost. *You know the one — with the wheel and the clay and Patrick Swayze's wonderful hands. That is to say, I think both you and your work are quite lovely and well worth the extra five minutes it takes for me to pass through your block before getting to the subway. I just thought you should know.*

Love,
Anon

With a sharp intake of breath, Rosie hit send and sipped the last dregs of her herbal tea before throwing the takeout cup into the nearest bin. She'd been wanting to post on the Don't Be a Stranger app for weeks, but as a marketing consultant for the brand itself, she was worried that her co-workers would somehow find out that user *LookingforLove* was her. Wade in particular would tease her to no end if he knew.

And then she'd grown more desperate, more

lonely, more in love with the majestic stranger behind the window by the day, and she'd needed an outlet — and maybe a decent bloody date. So she'd started responding to other people's posts for the sake of conversation, and then she'd given up on Tinder after a string of awful experiences, swapping it instead for where she was now: her very first blind date, acquired via Don't Be a Stranger.

She wended her way through Central Park with apprehension bubbling in her gut and her frostbitten fingers clutching the strap of her shoulder bag for dear life. She didn't even know *who* she was looking for, only that she was supposed to meet them at Bethesda Fountain — which she found completely frozen over along with the algae-infested lake behind it as she stepped out of the shadows of the arches onto the slippery terrace.

The problem was that there were at least a dozen people lingering by the fountain, their faces glued to phones and their hot coffees steaming in gloved hands. Why she had planned a date outdoors in the dead of winter, Rosie didn't know. She supposed it was just further proof of how utterly desperate she was.

The person closest to her in age was a handsome businessman in a suit — *not somebody in need of a blind date*, she thought, *and certainly not someone with the username PretzelLover89*. His wedding band blinked against the low sun as he slid on a pair of leather gloves, and it was all the confirmation she needed.

Rosie tried to appear casual and composed as she strolled around the fountain, skipping over a teenager and an elderly man before coming to a pretty, dark-haired woman half-concealed by a thick woollen scarf. Her eyes, cast down like everybody else's, were accentuated with black liner, and her ears pointed in an elfin sort of way. Hope glowed in Rosie's chest, and she stepped forward tentatively.

"Er, *PretzelLover89*?"

The woman lifted her head with a frown. "Excuse me?"

Embarrassment sent Rosie rocking back on her heels. "Nothing. Sorry. I thought you were someone else." She puffed out a visible, curling breath and took a seat on the opposite side of the fountain, watching a horse-drawn carriage trot by. Behind it, in the middle of the terrace, a bearded man created large, rainbow-streaked bubbles with two sticks and a bucket of soapy water.

One of the bubbles drifted towards Rosie. She watched it wistfully, the child within her tempted to pop it with her nail. But then a wobbly face appeared behind it, and the bubble floated into the crisp, blue December sky to reveal a middle-aged, gangly man wearing... well. Rosie could only describe it as a clown suit, with a polka dot red bow tie and a yellow jacket. White and red makeup caked his face and his mousy brown hair was wilted — probably by the curly wig clutched in his hands.

Oh, God. No, thank you. Move along, sir. Don't let it be you, please... Rosie cringed and pretended to look interested in the man with the bubbles, praying the clown would wander off. She didn't fancy dating Pennywise's slightly friendlier cousin.

"Excuse me. Are you *LookingforLove*?"

Bollocks. He was either her blind date or just incredibly perceptive. Rosie clutched the lip of the fountain and forced a smile. "Aren't we all?"

The clown laughed raucously as though still in character and took a seat beside her. If Rosie hadn't had a fear of clowns before, that was set to change now. She shuffled down the fountain to put some space between them as who she assumed was *PretzelLover89* rambled on. "Sorry about the get-up. Just came from a kid's party. I had to fill in for a colleague."

Rosie arched an eyebrow. He hadn't even changed his shoes, and the gargantuan ones on his feet kicked her shins as he shifted. Feeling suddenly guilty, she told herself to stop being so judgemental. This was a blind date after all, and appearances meant nothing to her. He could be a nice, kind person; he could maybe even be exactly who she'd been looking for. And he was interesting, at least. "So... You're a clown?"

"We prefer the term 'entertainer'," he corrected wryly. "Oh, that reminds me. I brought something for you." *PretzelLover89* rooted through his oversized pockets, pulling out a sunflower.

With her heart fluttering, Rosie relaxed. Sunflowers were her favourite, and anybody who brought her a gift on a first date was surely a decent person. She supposed hings weren't so dire after all. "I didn't even know sunflowers were still in season. Thank —"

A spurt of cold water gushed into her mouth, drowning away her gratitude. She startled, her hand flying to her lips in confusion, only to find *PretzelLover89* doubled over. He clutched a red pump in his gloved hand, and it was connected to the sunflower by a rubber tube. "You should see your face! Oh, that was funny!"

Rosie might have laughed once. She might have stuck it out. But this was her fifth bad date since moving to New York three months ago, and all of her past relationships ended with her feeling belittled and humiliated, always the butt of the joke. Most of her days, she was on the verge of tears, homesick and depressed by the prospect of spending Christmas alone for the first time ever, an ocean away from everything she'd ever known and loved.

She didn't want to date a clown. She already played the part enough herself on a daily basis.

"Actually, I've just remembered that I need to get back to work," she lied, standing up and smoothing down her dress. "I have a big meeting later on to prepare for. I'll, er, text you, shall I?"

"But you don't have my number!" the clown called behind her.

She waved his words away and scuttled past the man and his bubbles, through the shadows of the stone arches. "Yes, okay! Bye!"

Rosie ran halfway through Central Park just to be sure the clown hadn't followed her. It was like a reenactment of an early birthday party she had worked hard to forget, when Ronald McDonald had accidentally stepped on her toe, popped her balloons, and then purposely stolen her McChicken Nuggets. Only when the skyscrapers grew closer again beyond the leafless trees did she come to a stop, slumping onto a frost-covered bench with tears welling in her eyes. This was it then. She was destined to be alone forever, and worse still was that she was alone in New York.

She shouldn't have moved here. She shouldn't have taken the bloody job. She'd been quite happy in Manchester, surrounded by semi-decent but perhaps slightly superficial friends and going home to her mum and dad's every weekend for a Sunday roast.

God, she missed her Sunday roasts. They didn't do them right here — she'd tried plenty of carveries. There were no Yorkshire puddings, for starters, and they could never get the gravy thick or rich enough.

Stretching out her thermal tights-covered legs, she tried to find some solace in the melodic notes floating from the violinist nearby and whipped out her phone again. She'd have to go back to work soon.

As much as she hated herself for it, Rosie opened Don't Be a Stranger. Sometimes, when she was feeling particularly desolate, she liked to read other users' postings about the people they'd fallen in love with, whether it be a short instant between strangers like her infatuation with the potter, or people who were no longer strangers going on their first, second, or third dates.

Her thumb stilled over one post in particular, written by someone named *TequilaQueen.*

Wanted: temporary Christmas date. Must be cute, no older than forty, and willing to pretend to be in a relationship for the sake of nosy, judgmental dad. Payment: homemade Christmas dinner. Must come equipped with pumpkin pie and vodka. Any and all genders welcome.

Rosie frowned, wiping her runny nose with the back of her glove. It wasn't quite the fairytale romance she'd spent every day since the age of thirteen — when she'd watched *10 Things I Hate About You* for the first time, thus triggering the first of many bouts of pansexual panic on account of her love for both Heath Ledger and Julia Stiles — hoping for, but... it would get her out of her dreary little apartment on Christmas.

No. It would be a new low, agreeing to fake date somebody just so she wouldn't have to be alone. What if they were like *PretzelLover89*, or her many brief encounters with awful people? She couldn't risk another experience like this one.

Still. *What if* it was different? Pretend dating always ended well in films, didn't it? What if Rosie had to keep trying, persevering, and this was her next chance to meet the person of her dreams? It was already a new approach, a new chance, and if the person turned out to be awful, she'd never have to see them again.

Rosie's numb fingers typed out a reply:

@LookingforLove: *Will shop-bought pumpkin pie do?*

With both dread and excitement fizzing in her chest, Rosie slipped her phone away and made her way back to work. When she was back at her desk, though, she couldn't help but check for a response.

Sure enough, she'd already gotten one.

@TequilaQueen: *Depends on the buyer. Let's do a trial run. Lunch tomorrow. Molly's Cupcakes on Bleecker St?*

It was on the opposite side of town to her office, but impulse drove Rosie to reply right away.

@LookingforLove: *See you then.*

She added a cupcake emoji for good measure and then locked her phone when Wade, her co-worker, appeared over her shoulder to gossip about a celebrity she'd never heard of before.

This meant she had no time to overthink it.

Three

@HopelessPoet: This poem is dedicated to the guy who gets on the subway every morning at 8.15 a.m., West Fourth Street, with a cream cheese and roast tomato bagel in hand.

*I am lactose intolerant
and yet I would risk it all
for a bite of your breakfast,
for a bite of conversation.
I find myself thinking of you
in the soup aisle,
thinking if you are tomato soup,
then I am chicken (cluck, cluck, cluck)
because I'll never be brave enough
to try to meet your eye.
Enjoy your bagel, stranger of my heart,
while I enjoy our silent rides through tunnels of black,
knowing the quiet darkness is all we'll ever have.*

Arden shook her head, a line sinking in the space between her brows. This app was... weird. She'd downloaded it out of sheer curiosity after Quinn had mentioned it, but so far, all she'd found was strangers going into a concerning amount of detail about their fleeting crushes on people they didn't know — using bad poetry now, too. It had caused her to hold off creating an account. If somebody ever wrote about her like that, she might have considered reporting it to the police and taking out a restraining order so she didn't dare take the risk.

With an impatient sigh, she closed the app and went back into her texts to see where Quinn was. She was used to her sister's tardiness, but thirty-eight minutes and counting was a tad ridiculous. Arden had things to do, vases to make, clay to mould and fire. And those cupcakes at the front of the bakery, behind a glass counter, were staring at her. She was starving, and her thrice-refilled mug of coffee was doing nothing to satisfy her grumbling stomach.

She was just about to cave and buy something when the bell above the front door tinkled out. Relief rushed through Arden, but it was quickly diminished when she saw the woman who had stepped inside.

A dark-haired, red-lipped stranger with choppy bangs falling into her eyes stepped into the store. Not Quinn. Arden slumped back into her seat and balanced her chin in her palm. She'd give Quinn five more minutes, after that, she was leaving.

The woman who had just come in glanced around warily, the entire bakery and its six seated customers grazed by murky green eyes. And then she huffed, her arms slapping to her sides as she called, "Tequila queen?"

Arden frowned at that. Was she making a statement? Naming *herself* the tequila queen? This didn't seem like the right place to do it, what with it being a weekday lunchtime and them being in an alcohol-free bakery. Maybe she was already drunk.

She lowered her attention to risk making eye contact with the strange, drunk woman. She pulled out her phone to text Quinn.

Arden: *Where are you? Think we should eat somewhere else. Some weirdo just came in announcing herself to be the queen of tequila. Also, hurry up, asswipe!*

Quinn: *Oh, yeah, about that... I'm not coming. Also, she's not a weirdo. She's Don't Be a Stranger user @LookingforLove and she is your fake Christmas date. Enjoy! Is she hot? Did I choose wisely? Will Dad approve? Tell me everything later!*

It took a long time for Arden to process Quinn's words, gathered in a green bubble on the screen. So long, in fact, that the woman had taken to asking every customer individually if they were a tequila queen.

Arden gritted her teeth. She could say no. Make a run for it. Leave the woman to think that she'd been stood up. But that wasn't fair. Other than the vibrant colours she wore and the fact that she seemed to lack any sense of social etiquette or dignity, she seemed okay. Younger than Arden maybe, but... well, pretty. Not Arden's usual type, but certainly somebody she'd remember if they passed her in the street.

The woman finally made it to Arden's table, her round eyes desperate and doe-like as she clutched her gloves and asked, "Are *you* TequilaQueen?"

Arden sucked in a long breath, tilting her chin to look at the woman properly. "No."

The woman's features fell, the rest of her frame wilting with them, and guilt forced Arden's next words from her mouth.

"But my sister is, I assume." Arden wiggled the unlocked phone, still displaying Quinn's messages, in front of her. "Seems I've been set up... Are you *LookingforLove*?"

Colour bled back into the woman's features, her cheeks turned rosy and her lips curled into a striking, gap-toothed smile. "That's me. May I...?"

Her accent was elegant and soft-vowelled, British, reminding Arden of a less brutish *Game of Thrones* character. She motioned hesitantly to the chair opposite. "Of course."

"Thank you." The woman sat, shuffling so much that the chair legs screeched their protest against the tiles. "I, er... I'm Rosie." She extended a hand expectantly.

Arden took it. It was perhaps the most awkward, clammy handshake she'd ever been a part of and she pulled back quickly to wipe her palm on her jeans. "Arden."

"So... You're *not TequilaQueen*?"

"No. No. My sister made that post on Don't

Be a Stranger for me against my will. I was sort of hoping nothing would come of it. And then she told me to meet her here and, well... "

Rosie grimaced. "Sorry."

"It's not your fault." But it *was* Quinn's. Arden wouldn't let this one go too easily. She was mortified, to say the least, her face searing with heat.

"So... you're not looking for a date, then?"

"I..." Arden chewed on her bottom lip, clutching her coffee mug as though it could save her from the uncomfortable conversation. It didn't, and she had an answer to give. She just didn't know what it should be. She'd lied to her dad about dating, and now...

Now she was here, sitting across from a stranger, and she had two options.

"A fake date, I should say," Rosie continued wryly. "That's what your sister called it, anyway."

The fact that she knew what she was getting into soothed Arden's frayed nerves just slightly, leaving her to shrink lower into her chair. She could pretend to date Rosie for a night, couldn't she? To please her dad and show her family that she wasn't completely and utterly pathetic... To prove to them that she was over Josh and to prevent any future conversations about him...

She shouldn't have felt as though she *had* to prove anything, but she did — if only to stop feeling fractured and ashamed every time her dad brought up her love life.

"Right." Arden nodded, scrutinising Rosie once more. She *was* very pretty. Different. Bubbly. Her dad would be happy, and she was certainly the furthest from Josh that Arden could have found. But if Arden did agree, what would be in it for Rosie? "If you don't mind me asking, why would you agree to something like this? I mean… it's a little strange. I know why *I* need a 'fake date'," she used air quotations, feeling slightly — *very* — immature for saying the words aloud, "but why do you? Don't you have better ways to spend Christmas Day?"

"Well… no." Rosie shrugged, her features flickering with something solemn. It came and went so quickly, Arden didn't have time to read into it. "My family is in the UK, and I only just moved here so I don't have many friends. If I'm being honest, this seemed like a good way of passing the time."

"Passing the time?" Arden repeated, raising an eyebrow.

"I get lonely." Rosie made the confession without so much as blinking, though her eyes sparkled with the promise of tears. "I've been on the app for a while now, but dating isn't working out the way I'd hoped. Maybe I could do with a day of pretending."

Sympathy welled in Arden. New York was a lonely place, even with family not too far away. There were so many people here that she'd long since stopped noticing their faces. Everyone was anonymous. Everyone was no one at all.

It had gotten worse after the divorce. Without a hand to hold, the traffic-clogged streets felt darker, longer. The skyscrapers looked taller as they cast ominous shadows. She couldn't have imagined what it must have felt like for someone so far from home, especially over the holidays.

Arden tucked a golden, wavy strand of hair behind her ear and nodded. "I get that. Nobody should have to spend Christmas alone."

"What about you?" Rosie seemed to snap out of her heartache all at once, straightening in her chair. "Why do you need someone to pretend to date you? I'm sure you could get anyone you wanted."

"I don't *need* someone," Arden said, growing hot from the compliment. "But... well, my dad worries about me. I got a divorce about a year ago, and he's concerned because I've not dated since. It's not that I can't find anybody new — I just haven't tried. But it's getting exhausting to have to deal with a million questions, and then the rest of the relatives join in, too. They don't get that I'm okay on my own, and they make me feel like maybe I *shouldn't* be. Like it's tragic."

"Ah, yes. My cousin always used to try to set me up with the neighbour when she came around for Christmas dinner." The hint of a smile dimpled at the corner of Rosie's mouth.

"What is it with families?" A frustrated laugh slipped from Arden, forgetting for a moment that she was talking to a stranger, or otherwise a potential pretend girlfriend. "They have to stick their nose in and act like you've lost a limb if you're single."

"It's bloody exhausting." Rosie wrinkled her freckled nose in agreement. "The world doesn't revolve around relationships, for Christ's sake."

"Exactly! I'm fine on my own." Arden crossed her arms over her chest and realised, for the first time, that she meant it. She *was* fine. It was difficult sometimes, but the world hadn't stopped turning without Josh in it. In fact, she no longer had to pretend to enjoy takeout from that shitty Italian place on the block next to his penthouse apartment, or pick up dirty socks from under the bed, or fight over the bathroom in the morning. She was fine. And finer still because finally, someone understood. Because, finally, she'd opened up about her divorce and hadn't been met with sombre glances or suggestions of potential dates. She wasn't less of a person for being on her own, and she never should have been made to feel like one.

Rosie's smile fell gradually. She licked her lips, fiddling with the sugar pot in the middle of the table. "So... I suppose that means you won't be needing a date, then?"

"Well..." Arden didn't *need* a date to be happy, but... she did need everybody to lay off the sympathy and constant talk of her barren love life. Taking Rosie sounded better than the alternative if it meant one day without it all. And Rosie seemed okay. Nice, even. She didn't deserve to spend the holidays alone. They'd be doing each other a favour. "I wouldn't say that. If we're both in need of company…"

Rosie blew out a breath of relief. "Good because I already bought the pie."

Arden couldn't help but laugh, leaning forward without really noticing.

"So…" Rosie said. "What's next? Do we get to know each other over a few cupcakes? You know… to make it believable?"

Arden hadn't really thought about what would come next, but she realised now that if they wanted to sell this, they'd have to at least know enough about one another to appear like they were close. As it stood, Arden knew absolutely nothing about Rosie other than the fact that she was British and — judging by the way her eyes kept slipping back to the cake displays — as hungry as Arden was.

"I guess we do. If you don't have time, though…"

"Nah, it's fine. If my boss asks, I'm working from home today. I'm going to have to sample that red velvet cupcake." Rosie was already wandering towards the display of desserts, her striped skirt swishing beneath a long coat. "Then again, I do love a good cheesecake…"

With something strange fluttering in her chest, Arden leaned back in her chair. Maybe she wouldn't have to kill her sister after all.

∞∞∞

"So…" Rosie swiped a lump of butterscotch frosting from her mouth, trying to chew her cupcake quickly so that she could learn more about Arden. She couldn't really believe her luck. She'd been expecting somebody like the clown she'd met in Central Park yesterday. But Arden was easy to talk to once Rosie had looked past her intimidating beauty, and she couldn't find anything wrong with her… yet, at least. In fact, she was too perfect for Rosie. Too composed and independent and focused.

Arden hummed expectantly, civilised enough to eat her slice of lemon and ginger cake with a fork. Not like Rosie, who had just shoved the food in. She'd forgotten to have breakfast this morning, and she was making up for it now. She was two cupcakes and a cheesecake down and still counting.

"Tell me about you. I need to know who I'm supposed to be dating. What do you do for work?"

Arden cleared her throat and placed down her fork, swiping her cascading blonde waves off one shoulder. "I own a pottery studio in the East Village. I make my own stuff to sell but also run classes for anyone who wants to learn."

Rosie froze, her sticky, crumbling cake

sitting heavy on her tongue. She swallowed it down slowly, trying not to choke, and then examined Arden again.

It was always difficult to make out the pretty potter Rosie passed every morning on her way to the subway station. With Christmas lights dangling in the windows and the early morning sunrise usually glaring off the glass, she only knew that the woman inside was blonde and soft-figured like Rosie, and she usually sat with a pottery wheel between her legs. But anything else Rosie had liked, she'd made up about the woman herself in her drifting daydreams.

It couldn't have been her. It was too much of a coincidence. But here Rosie was, sitting in a bakery not *too* far from East 12th Street, opposite a potter who owned a studio in her village.

"The one on East 12th Street?" Rosie asked cautiously.

Surprise sparkled in Arden's cornflower-blue eyes. "You know it?"

"I pass it every morning on my way to work." *And stare at you through the window like a gormless idiot.* Heat kindled in Rosie's chest. How many times had she admired Arden? How many times had they crossed paths without knowing? And now she was here, and so was Rosie. Either the universe was playing games with her, or... it was fate.

"No way." Arden's features crumpled with disbelief, and her elbows shuffled further across the table. Closer to Rosie. Instinctively, Rosie inched forward, too, her palms trickling with sweat and her pulse thrumming through her veins. And then Arden sat back again, passing cake crumbs around her plate with the tines of her fork absently, and whatever moment of serendipity they'd just shared ebbed. "Anyway, what about you? What was worth moving halfway across the world for?"

"I don't know if it was worth it," Rosie said, "But a job offer. I actually work on the marketing team for Don't Be a Stranger."

Arden's brows rose. "The app?"

Rosie nodded, smirking. "Yep. Don't tell my co-workers, though. They'll never let me live it down."

"So you're actually using it... like, for dating?" A hint of judgement laced Arden's words, leaving Rosie to frown uneasily. There was nothing wrong with dating apps, and out of all of them, Don't Be a Stranger was by far the most interesting and the safest.

And besides, it was just... nice. Rosie liked being able to talk to people without them knowing who she was. She liked seeing strangers find common ground, sometimes even a spark, without even having seen one another's faces. It wasn't always good, but when things worked out, it was special.

"Trying to. It's not working out too well, clearly. You don't like it?"

Arden shrugged. "It just seems a little weird that everybody is anonymous. You could be talking to anyone."

"Actually, everyone has to provide extra information for security purposes and connect a private social media account — just in case they aren't who they say they are. We have a lot of people vetting the users behind the scenes. It's no more dangerous than any other dating site."

"Are they paying you to market it to me now?"

Rosie snorted. "No. I just... I like the app. I'm proud to work on it, really, even if it's only the marketing side of things. Don't you think it's a little bit beautiful?"

"That people can post about how obsessed they are with strangers without consequences?"

She fidgeted with her napkin, her skin prickling uncomfortably. Was that what she'd done by posting about the potter — Arden? Was it creepy to admire strangers? Everybody did it. Rosie had been falling in love with people on public transport since the age of thirteen. But were people not *supposed* to discuss those fleeting crushes? They felt so important, so worthy of discussing... now more than ever, since she'd met hers in the flesh today. Not that she'd want Arden to know. In fact, she'd probably delete the post as soon as she got home.

"Maybe not when you put it like that," Rosie said finally, swallowing down her unease. "But it's nice to see people connecting. Sometimes I just read the posts and replies, and if I see that they're meeting somewhere close by... well, I go, too. Just to see."

Oh, God. She shouldn't have admitted that. Her cheeks burned as Arden pursed her lips.

"You follow people to watch them meet?"

"Only if it's for the first time!" Rosie rushed to explain. "I just... I suppose I like to know that there are people out there falling in love. It gives me hope. I'd go insane if I only had my own experiences to go off. Let me show you..." She pulled out her phone and opened Don't Be a Stranger, scrolling through a few posts before one caught her eye. "Look. These two are about to meet in Washington Square Park."

"So... you want to go?" Arden bit her lip warily and worry began to claw at Rosie. It wasn't too late for Arden to back out of their Christmas arrangement. Had Rosie made an idiot of herself already and ruined it all?

"Well, we don't have to, but..." But she wanted to. She wanted Arden to understand, though she was still a stranger, too.

"I'll get another round of coffees to go, then." Arden stood up, smiling softly before heading over to the counter again. Rosie relaxed in her chair. She hadn't scared Arden away — *yet*.

But there was still plenty of time.

Four

@JustASmallTownBoy: _@PeppermintsForBreakfast_
meet me under Washington Square Arch at
two-thirty. It's about time I got to put a face
to the username. I'm all in if you are.

Yours,
Small Town Boy
(P.S. Bring peppermints. We're gonna need 'em.)

Arden perched on the edge of the park's grey
fountain, the sputtering water behind her an
unwelcome reminder of the amount of coffee she'd
consumed. It was hard to ignore since it was
now swishing in her bladder. It was a miserable
day, sleet showering the city in the cold, damp,
and grey in regular intervals, and nobody stood
beneath the arch yet. She checked her wristwatch
and found that there was still ten minutes to
go until *JustASmallTownBoy* was due to meet
PeppermintsForBreakfast.

This was not an event Arden would have

expected to witness today. Still, she couldn't suppress her smile when she looked at Rosie and found her jiggling excitedly, her eyes never leaving the arch.

Definitely not what Arden had expected today.

She tried to imagine Rosie in her family home out in Westhampton. Her eclectic, colourful dress against the white walls and ceiling to floor windows, and all of her dad's neatly arranged slate-grey furniture. Josh had fit in well there, in cardigans and loafers or suits if it was a special occasion, but Rosie... She was different. Not the sort of person Arden would usually date, though not in a bad way. It might take a little bit of convincing to make it believable, and they'd have to play off their animated stream of conversation and jokes rather than the things they had in common.

"I guess we need to establish a story for this... thing." Arden couldn't say what it really was. An act. Fake dating. It didn't make any sense to her yet and was perhaps the most bizarre scheme she'd ever engaged in. She never usually had to lie to her family. "People will have questions about us."

Rosie blew out a breath, strong enough to disrupt her bangs. She sat beside Arden and bundled her scarf around her chin, her nose pink and runny. "This is weird, isn't it?"

Arden choked on a laugh. "Honestly, I didn't

think people did this in real life."

"It could be fun, though. Beats eating takeout on my own. So, go on then. How did we meet?"

She contemplated this for a moment. Was she even any good at lying? She'd never really had to try. Quinn had always been much better at it, so if they were ever in trouble growing up, it was her who found a way out of it. Arden tried to stick to the truth. "We met in a bakery?"

"That's believable." Rosie smirked, nudging Arden with her elbow. The shifting traffic lights glowed behind her through the spurting water. "Who asked who on a date?"

"We were set up," Arden answered, glad to find that she hadn't had to come up with original material yet. "A mutual friend."

"You're good at this."

A trickle of warmth rushed through Arden, and she tucked her hair behind her ear coyly. "The closer we can keep it to the truth, the better, I guess."

"How long have we been dating? Are we exclusive?"

She shrugged, taking another sip of coffee despite her increasing need to pee. Why was she so nervous? It was only a game of pretend. "A month or so, maybe?"

"Two," Rosie amended, pulling out her phone and typing something. "Let's write it down in case we forget all this. My memory's like a sieve."

Arden peered over Rosie's shoulder, finding the notes app open with the title: **Arden and Rosie's Dating Story.**

"That reminds me," Rosie continued. "I should get your number." She offered out her phone, and Arden typed in her number quickly, with a silent prayer in the back of her mind that she was doing the right thing. Rosie could still turn out to be a creep who ended up blowing up Arden's phone or her apartment. But she supposed it was too late to back out now, and she didn't feel wary or unsure.

"You should also know about my family, I think." Arden passed the phone back as Rosie nodded.

"That's true. Who should I expect?"

"Well, Quinn, my sister... She's a pain in the ass and will probably find a way to turn the entire dinner into chaos. She looks like I would if I joined a grunge band and pierced my nose. And then there's my dad and his husband, Murray. They're nosy but harmless, and Dad will just be glad I'm dating somebody, so he shouldn't grill you too hard. Then there's the extended family. My Aunt Gina, her three kids, and my grandma will probably be there, too, as well as Murray's parents. Murray also has a son, Nathan, but most of the time he ignores our existence so don't feel bad if he spends the entire day giving you death stares across the table."

Rosie laughed, typing the information

frantically. "Thanks for the warning. Is there... Is there a certain way you want me to act? I wouldn't want to embarrass you or anything. Obviously, I'll be on my best behaviour."

Arden frowned. Rosie was different, yes, but the idea of her embarrassing Arden hadn't crossed her mind once. She wasn't messy and self-destructive like Quinn. She seemed the opposite, really. Like spring made flesh, with all the glorious chaos of a newborn lamb and all the bright colours of a garden in bloom. If she acted the way she had today, if this version of Rosie was the real one, then there was nothing wrong with her. "How would you embarrass me?"

"Well." Rosie cleared her throat, propping one leg over the other as she looked anywhere but at Arden. "I suppose I just do sometimes. You seem very... well-put-together. You dress like an adult, you own your own studio, and you clearly have a lot of life experience. I'm sort of a thirteen-year-old in a twenty-seven-year-old's body, I think. We don't really look the part, do we?"

A sharp pang shot through Arden though she couldn't work out why. Sympathy, perhaps? Or maybe she was wondering if Rosie had been told she was embarrassing before; if somebody in her past had made her feel that way.

"I like the dress," Arden admitted, and then, when her gaze fell to Rosie's rainbow-patterned Mary Janes, "*and* the shoes. Maybe we're different, but that's not a bad thing. Besides, if anyone

36

embarrasses me, it's my family. I don't see anything about you so far that would embarrass me — unless you don't like dogs. That would be tragic for my dad's pomeranian, Peaches."

"I'm usually a cat lady, but for Peaches, I'll reconsider," Rosie said. "Anything else I should know?"

Arden hummed in thought, but everything about home seemed to slip her mind beneath Rosie's gaze. If this were real, she wouldn't have to tell Rosie everything about her life now. They'd have time to learn about one another. They wouldn't be two strangers sitting by a fountain, treating families like pieces of homework.

But it wasn't real.

Before she could summon an answer, Rosie gasped and pointed without any sense of subtlety to the arch. "There they are!"

Arden followed her focus, finding two men standing in the shadow of the arch, toothy grins sparkling on their faces. From this distance, Arden couldn't make out what they were saying — but she didn't have to. After a few laughs, broken by passing traffic and keening cop car sirens, the couple leaned into one another. The taller one pulled something out of his pocket as their lips met. Arden squinted and realised it was the blue and white wrapper of peppermint-flavoured candy.

A laugh spilt from her without warning, and her breath hitched in her throat. Maybe Rosie was right. Maybe Arden needed a reminder today that, despite her divorce and non-existent dating life, love still existed. Love still waited. People found it every day.

She understood now why Rosie sometimes came to the places mentioned on the app to watch their stories unfold. The cold stung Arden's eyes as the men's hands interlocked and they began to wander away, their figures blurring with the rainy sidewalks and headlights.

"How sweet was that?" Rosie breathed wistfully beside Arden. Arden turned, finding Rosie teary, her chin wobbly. "See? Wasn't it nice to see two people find each other? I'm not a complete weirdo."

"Just a hopeless romantic." It was said without judgement or disapproval. Arden might have been alone and she might have given up on finding love again, but that didn't mean she wished the same for others. It was nice that some people were still naive enough to believe it could exist. The thorns that always followed the roses mustn't have touched Rosie yet.

"Maybe. Or maybe just a bit sad and lonely." Rosie smirked, though it didn't meet her eyes. "Anyway... what's the plan for getting there? Should I meet you there?"

"If you text me your address, I'll pick you up at eleven."

Rosie nodded, her eyes still glazed, unfocused. "Okay. Eleven. Sounds good. What about…" Her face flushed with colour, and she worried at her lip. "What about the other couple-y stuff? Hand holding and all that? Will we do that?"

Arden hadn't even thought of that. Clearly, she was an amateur in the field of fake relationships because it should have been the first thing they talked about. "I guess… it *would* make it more believable. We don't need to go over the top or anything though."

"Okay. Then… I'll hold your hand." Rosie said it so softly that Arden's heartbeat seemed to quieten just so that she could hear it. She was suddenly very aware of their gloved hands only inches apart — Arden's half-pressed beneath her numb thigh and Rosie's curled in the pocket of her coat. Is this how they would be at the dinner table? Two strangers who were not sure how to touch one another?

Maybe none of it would work. Maybe all of this was a mistake and Arden should just back out. She couldn't pretend to be in love with somebody she'd only met an hour ago, could she?

"I, er, have a lesson scheduled for three, so I should go." Arden stood before she could talk herself out of it and slung her purse back onto her shoulder, glad to get the blood moving through her veins again. Winter was a beast in New York City, and Arden was sick of feeling the cold gnaw through her bones. "If you have any questions or anything, you can text me. Or come see me in the studio, I guess."

"Oh... okay. I'll see you soon, then." Rosie rose from the fountain's edge too, shifting on hesitant feet as though not sure how to wish Arden a goodbye. Arden felt the same. A wave felt too casual, a handshake too formal, but a hug or a kiss on the cheek would be too much.

Arden settled on a bright smile. "See you soon," she agreed, and then wandered away to free herself from the sudden awkwardness. Her gut remained a tangled web of reservations and embarrassment — and perhaps a faint knot of excitement — and there was no ridding herself of it.

The act had been rehearsed. Now, she just had to make it through the dinner with Rosie at her side.

No big deal.

Five

@cottonheadedninnymuggins: the person i like just told me they hate the polar express and frankly i don't need that negativity in my life, so my search for love continues. anybody else an xmas movie fanatic? hmu. let's snuggle.

Nerves jangled through Rosie like rusty jingle bells as they rolled up to Arden's family home in Westhampton. Since the move, she'd never even left the city, and though it was refreshing to be surrounded by smooth landscapes and blue-grey shores rather than dull, towering skyscrapers, she still felt out of place — especially in Arden's car. The ride down had been a lot of small talk above the low Christmas songs that were droning repetitively from the radio. She'd called her mum this morning and had fought back tears, homesickness settling like a chunk of metal in her gut.

She missed Manchester. She missed familiarity. She missed home-cooked meals and watching *The Vicar of Dibley* re-runs with her dad while Mum huffed and puffed over lumpy gravy in the kitchen while refusing any offer of help. She could have gone back to the UK for a week if she'd wanted — the offer of working remotely when needed was always there — but she couldn't survive another eight hours of panic attacks and trying not to look out of the plane window to see how high she was, so she'd chosen to remain in the city alone, never quite sure when she'd see her family again.

At least she had something to preoccupy herself with now, though that "something was an intimidatingly colossal house that left her jaw hanging open in awe. Rosie didn't do fancy. She lived in an old apartment with leaky pipes and loose floorboards. Even her house back home was rented from the Council.

What was she doing here?

She couldn't quite remember.

Arden turned the engine off, leaving them blanketed in a thick silence. "You're not going to fake break up with me now, are you?"

"It's a very nice house," was all that Rosie could stutter out as she eyed the blindingly white pillars, neatly arranged shrubs, and the large garage with two shutters down.

"It is."

"And I have a ladder in my tights." Rosie lifted her knee to display the frayed hole. She'd only noticed halfway here that she'd thrown on the wrong pair this morning.

Arden tutted and tugged on the hem of Rosie's coral-red dress. The familiarity of the gesture left Rosie frozen in place. "Nobody will notice that. But if you don't want to do this…"

"No, I do," Rosie blurted quickly. What was she going to do if she backed out now? Sit in Arden's car while Arden went inside alone? Besides, her pumpkin pie was strapped in by a seatbelt in the backseat. She hadn't dared bring vodka even though Arden's sister had requested it.

Arden raised an eyebrow.

"It's just…" Rosie trailed off and skimmed over the Georgian colonial architecture again. "It's a very nice house."

"You've already said that," Arden pointed out.

Rosie chewed on her lip, her heart thundering in her chest. She was overwhelmed. Her palms were clammy. She had no idea why she was here or what she had gotten herself into. "Maybe I'm not classy enough to be your fake girlfriend."

With a scoff, Arden unfastened her seatbelt. "We're not classy people. My sister is a college dropout and will probably show up wearing ripped jeans. You're already miles ahead of her. Besides, you have a fancy British accent. That has to count for something."

"So I don't need to know what a salad fork is?"

"No. We are not snooty fork people." Arden

reached across the gearstick, her hand falling onto Rosie's thigh. Rosie looked down in surprise as Arden's warmth tingled through her. "You'll be fine, Rosie. They'll love you. Promise."

Rosie wasn't sure how Arden knew that being as she barely even knew *her*, but the words set her at ease all the same. "Okay." She loosed a jagged breath and unfastened her seatbelt. "I suppose it's time to go in, then."

"I suppose it is." Arden got out of the car, and Rosie followed, collecting her pie from the backseat. Somehow, it had survived the trip — probably better than Rosie had, considering the holes in her clothes. Under her breath, she muttered the names Arden had left in the **Arden and Rosie's Dating Story** note on her phone. She'd been memorising them all week. "Dad is James Gunderson. Step-dad is Murray Gunderson. Step-dad's son is Nathan Gunderson. Sister is Quinn, AKA *TequilaQueen*. Aunt is —"

"*Rosie*," Arden interrupted, halting at the foot of the steps leading to the porch. Her fingers curled around the cuff of Rosie's sleeve, forcing her to stop as well. The jolt caused the pie to slide about in its tray, and in a moment of panic, left Rosie clutching it tighter. "Relax. They're going to think you're some robotic fact dispenser I made because I was too pathetic to find a real person."

Rosie sagged in defeat and smoothed down her unruly hair a final time. "Sorry. I just... I've never done anything like this before."

"Neither have I, believe it or not." Arden's fingers slipped between Rosie's and it was warm and smooth and comforting. It had been a long time since anybody had held Rosie's hand. She didn't know what to do until Arden dragged her up the steps and onto the porch. Beneath the portico, illuminated by a hanging lantern between them, they exchanged nervous glances and sucked in a synchronised breath.

"Shall we?" asked Arden.

Rosie nodded and swallowed down her anxiety, though her stomach remained a tight knot.

Before Arden could knock, the door swung open.

∞∞∞

It was Murray, Arden's step-dad, who greeted them at the door, all gummy smile and slicked-back silver hair.

Arden forced a grin of her own and clutched Rosie's hand tighter. "Merry Christmas!"

"Arden!" Murray glanced between them, curiosity glinting in his dark eyes as he extended a hand to Rosie. "And you must be our esteemed guest. James has talked non-stop about how excited he is to meet you!"

Rosie pulled away from Arden to shake his hand and then offered out the pumpkin pie. "If I'd have known your house was this big, I would have brought a fancier pie." She laughed nervously, her rosy, freckled cheeks swelling.

"This looks good to me." Murray stepped aside to invite them in, and Arden breathed a sigh of relief when she stepped into the warmth of her own house. The rich aroma of garlic-lathered turkey and spiced vegetables greeted them: the smell of Christmas, home. Not the one she'd grown up in, but the one that had become a safe place after her dad had left her mom.

Murray led them through the tinsel-covered hall into the kitchen. Family photographs hung on every wall as though it was a gallery, and her mom was in none of them. It sent a pang of sadness through Arden. She didn't even know where her mom was now. It had been years since the last time they'd spoken. She only hoped that Quinn would quit while she was ahead before she ended up the same way.

In the kitchen, her dad hovered between the oven and the stove, mashing potatoes and shaking baking trays of roasted carrots and cauliflower to keep them from sticking to the bottom. He stopped when he noticed them; his features illuminating with joy. "You made it!"

"Always do." Arden walked straight into his arms, her eyes fluttering closed as he placed a kiss in her hair. "Merry Christmas, Dad. This is Rosie…" She trailed off as she pulled away, realising only then that she didn't know Rosie's surname. Not that it mattered. Not that they would ask... she hoped.

"Rosie." Her dad repeated her name as though it was a revelation, his cheeks dimpling as he drew her into a hug without shame or hesitance. Rosie's arms hovered awkwardly at his back, and Arden winced her apology when their eyes met. "It's so good to meet you. Arden's been keeping you a secret!"

"Thank you for inviting me into your home," Rosie replied politely, looking dishevelled when Arden's dad finally loosened his grip. "It's very lovely."

Before her dad could reply, Quinn wandered into the kitchen — barefoot and looking as though she'd just been dragged through a bush. Her boyfriend, Leo, followed close behind, an oily smile curling across an unshaven face. Arden clamped down on her upper lip before it curled into an instinctive sneer. Out of all of Quinn's shitty choices, Leo was the shittiest so far, and Arden was certain that he was the reason her partying had gotten worse over the last few months.

"Arden," he remarked.

"Leo." Her reply was clipped, and she crossed her arms over her chest. "Quinn. Merry Christmas."

"And a crappy New Year." Quinn headed straight to the fridge to pull out a bottle of white wine. She didn't bother to find a glass, instead uncorking it with her teeth and gulping it down straight from the bottle. "Oh, hey!" Her eyes widened as she noticed Rosie. "You're her!"

"Quinn." Their dad tutted and rolled his eyes. "That's not the way to greet your sister's new girlfriend."

"Sorry." Quinn's lips twitched with a knowing smirk. "Glad you're not a creepy old man, anyways. I had my doubts."

"So am I," Rosie said.

So was Arden, but pointing it out in front of half her family wasn't ideal. She rolled her eyes, glad when their dad placed his pan of potatoes back on the stove and threw a tea towel over his shoulder, saying, "Rosie. Why don't I give you a tour of the place?"

"Oh..." Rosie shifted nervously, and Arden didn't have time to warn her that she wouldn't get a choice. Her dad was already pulling her out of the kitchen by the hand, into the dining room. Leo took a fistful of dry roasted peanuts from a bowl and then followed aimlessly. Quinn made to leave, too, but Arden tugged her back.

"Can you just not be..." Arden gestured to Quinn, unable to find the right words to describe her, "you," she settled on, "today?"

Quinn placed a hand to her chest as though offended. "What's that supposed to mean?"

"It means let's just have a nice Christmas. No drama or arguments or causing a scene when you get too drunk to stand."

She rolled her eyes, ringed by smudged eyeliner. "You make me sound like Mom."

Arden said nothing, though the words rolled about on her tongue all the same. *You are.*

"Anyway." With another glug of wine, Quinn seated herself on an island stool. "Can we talk about your new girlfriend? She looks like Velma from *Scooby-Doo.*"

"Don't be a bitch, Quinn."

"I'm not! Velma is hot as fuck. Maybe you'll end up..." Quinn mashed her fingers together crudely, "You know. Actually together. And it will be all because of me, your wonderful matchmaking sister."

Arden yanked on her sister's knotted hair, and then shoved her for good measure, too. "Don't think you're off the hook for setting me up."

"Whatever. You'll be thanking me later."

Scoffing, Arden made her way out of the kitchen to save Rosie from whatever interrogation her dad was bestowing upon her. "And brush your hair," she called over her shoulder. "It looks like a bird's nest."

"Well, your ass looks flat as a pancake in that dress!" Quinn retorted. Arden only shot her the middle finger, though her snipes would always be born from concern. She didn't want to lose her sister — to alcohol, to Leo, to whatever shadow had been perched on her shoulder for so long.

And maybe, secretly, she *was* glad that Quinn had set her up with Rosie at the bakery last week. She'd been in the house for approximately five minutes and had received only positive greetings. No "Where's your date?" or "Still single, Ard?" or "Meet anyone new recently?" No sympathetic glances or pitying pats on the back as they ask "and how are *you* doing?" as though the answer will, inevitably, be "awful." Everybody was happy, including Arden.

She just hoped the rest of the day would run as smoothly.

Six

@SingleMomLife: My flight home got delayed by seven hours. I was convinced my Christmas was a lost cause until a life-ruiningly handsome man sitting next to me offered to buy me lunch. We haven't stopped talking since AND he lives in my city AND he wasn't put off by the fact I have kids. Everything happens for a reason, ya'll. Merry damn Christmas to me.

Rosie was glad that Arden's dad talked enough for both of them. She followed James around the house, breathless from the several flights of stairs, as he gushed about the newly installed jacuzzi in the sparkling-white guest bathroom and the study Murray had designed himself. She wasn't sure what pearly realm she'd stepped into and kept searching for signs of cameras as though she was on an episode of *Keeping Up with the Kardashians*, especially when Peaches the Pomeranian scuttled around her feet in the living room, her fluffy haircut tidier than Rosie's.

"So…" James finally stopped by the roaring fireplace, tucking his hands into the pockets of his slacks as Rosie fussed over the yapping dog. "Tell me about you, Rosie. Have you lived here long?"

"Three months," she answered, straightening again as her focus slipped to a set of silver-framed photographs on the mantel. The Christmas tree lights twinkled in her periphery, casting the room in a haze of buttery light that reminded her of Christmas Eves spent in fleecy pyjamas, watching *Home Alone,* and sipping hot chocolate from her mother's soup bowl-sized mugs. For once, the memory didn't fill her with an instant wave of homesickness. She still missed home, but... she was cosy here as well. Welcome. She was out of her miserable old apartment and among... well, strangers. But still. It was nice. She was even warming to Peaches, who now joined Leo on the couch in the hopes of catching one of the peanuts he was busy throwing into his mouth.

"Not long, then. How are you finding the Big Apple so far?" James's arm brushed hers, his eyes falling across the photographs too. Rosie assumed that the two blonde children sitting in an inflatable paddling pool in the first one were Quinn and Arden as babies, and there was another of James and Murray looking dapper and beaming on what must have been their wedding day, plus a group photo with all four of them and another couple Rosie hadn't met yet with sunlight flooding past them.

"Big," Rosie admitted. "Busy, too. But... I'm warming up to it."

"Maybe my daughter has something to do with that." The corner of his eyes wrinkled as he smiled, and a pang of guilt lanced through Rosie. Every bit of him *dripped* with happiness for Arden's new relationship, and it was all a lie. He'd welcomed Rosie into his home and made her feel like part of the family in just a short space of time. For the first time since they'd planned this, it felt like what it was: deceit. A rotten one that left Rosie's stomach churning.

"Maybe." Rosie forced herself to return his smile.

"Oh! I need to go and check on dinner. Murray's useless in the kitchen. Can I get you a drink?"

"Just water would be great. Thank you."

James squeezed her shoulder before he left, crossing paths with Arden at the door and planting a kiss on her forehead. Arden's returned grin didn't quite meet her eyes, and Rosie wondered if she felt bad too.

"Leo," Arden barked. "Stop letting Peaches eat peanuts."

"Woah. Chill." Leo raised his hands in surrender and then scoffed down another handful of nuts. "Where's your sister?"

"Setting the table. Go and help her, please."

Arden might as well have asked him to give up a lung for all the huffing and puffing it resulted in as he thrust himself out of the armchair and wandered off. "Great."

"You survived," she remarked to Rosie once they were alone, replacing her father's presence at Rosie's side. "I'm impressed."

Rosie laughed softly. "He wasn't that bad. Just excited. It's nice that he's so supportive of you. He reminds me of my dad."

"What would you be doing if you were at home now?"

Rosie shrugged, though she already knew the answer. Their Christmases were always the same: spent at home with too much tipple and definitely too many pigs in blankets — the sausage and bacon sort, not the rubbish pastry ones that Americans claimed them as here. "Well, we're five hours ahead, so we would have already eaten. We'd probably be too stuffed to move and end up lounging on the couch, watching a repeat of *Only Fools and Horses* because it's Dad's favourite. And Mum would be complaining because she wanted to watch *Chitty Chitty Bang Bang* on another channel, and Dad would probably let her because he's a pushover, but then Cousin Gillian would turn up with all her rowdy kids to shatter the peace, and we'd all get a bit pissed from Buck's Fizz just to deal with the noise."

Arden snorted. "I have no idea what most of that means, but it sounds perfect."

"It is." A lump clogged in Rosie's throat, and she searched frantically for a way to change the conversation before she ended up crying. "Who's the bloke next to you here?"

She pointed to the couple she'd noticed earlier. The man was fair-haired and square-jawed like Arden and Quinn and broad-shouldered and handsome like James. It wasn't a surprise, then, when Arden replied, "My brother, Tristan. That's his wife." She gestured to the pretty brunette woman standing beside him, a hint of sadness seeped into her tone. "They live in Australia now."

"You must miss him."

Arden hummed and then sucked in a sharp breath, drifting from whatever memory she'd been lost in. "Anyway. I think dinner is almost ready, and the other guests just got here. You should come and meet the rest of the family."

Rosie nodded and tried her best to ignore the disappointment guttering like a low-wicked candle in her stomach. Not because she didn't want to meet Arden's family, but because, for just a moment, she'd been content to talk to Arden, and it hadn't felt forced. It hadn't felt like an act. It hadn't felt like a lie.

Still, she followed Arden out into the dining room, instantly overwhelmed by all the new faces that had arrived since she'd toured the house. Faces that she would have to impress, just as she had James.

It was soon becoming exhausting, but Rosie fixed her friendliest smile, accepted Arden's outstretched hand, and plunged herself into the barrage of introductions and questions before she lost her nerve. She supposed it was good practice for any real relationships in her future — if she ever got that far.

∞∞∞∞

Anger brewed in the pit of Arden's stomach as she eyed her sister across the table, and the fingers her wrist was locked in. While the rest of the family ate and laughed, Leo and Quinn were having a not so subtle argument triggered when their dad had asked whether Quinn would ever consider going back to college. The answer, much to everybody's surprise, had been yes, and Leo hadn't seemed too happy about it. Arden despised the way he laid his hands on her like that. With his knuckles turning white, it was sure to leave bruises.

She cleared her throat and asked tersely, "Quinn. Pass the mashed potatoes, please?"

Finally, Leo released Quinn's wrist so that she could push over the large bowl of food. Arden glowered at Leo, half-tempted to say something, but it never worked. Everybody else ignored it, including their dad. Quinn didn't see how badly she was being treated, or maybe she did and had long since stopped caring.

"Thank you," Arden said finally, spooning a heap of mashed potatoes she didn't even want onto her plate.

"So, Arden," Aunt Gina began in her shrill

voice. Beside her, her five-year-old daughter, Jolie, had taken to using her hands to shovel peas into her mouth, and Aunt Gina gave her a light pat on the hand to stop her. "I feel like we haven't caught up in so long. I didn't even know you were dating again."

"Well, it's only been a few months." Arden cast a soft, sidelong smile to Rosie, who was twirling her fork aimlessly around her plate beside her. It was more difficult to lie at the table, with all eyes turned to her. Even Leo and Quinn had stopped bickering in hushed whispers and now stared.

"What about Joshua, Murray?" Aunt Gina asked. "Is he dating again, too?"

Murray pursed his lips into a thin line before sipping — *gulping* — his sparkling wine. He still shared a bond with Arden's ex-husband since he'd been the one to introduce them in the first place. Josh was Murray's colleague and friend, and Arden hadn't expected Murray to cease communicating with him after the divorce. Still, his name was never usually brought up at the table. She liked to keep it all separate, and so did he. Aunt Gina, on the other hand, had never been one to show much tact.

"Out of respect for my step-daughter, I don't tend to ask Josh about his love life, Gina," Murray said finally. Beside him, his mom frowned, probably having no idea who Josh was. Arden only saw the elderly woman every blue moon, and it had been a surprise that she'd turned up to dinner. Her own gran had cancelled last minute with complaints of the flu — a fact Arden wasn't too disappointed about.

"Still, it must be weird, dating again." Aunt Gina sawed her turkey and then glanced at Rosie. "What's your name again? Ronnie?"

"Rosie," Rosie answered politely.

Arden sighed, her patience fraying. She'd brought Rosie here so that she *wouldn't* have to talk about her divorce.

"Right. Rosie. Rosie doesn't seem like your usual type, Arden. What's her line of work?"

"I'm a marketing specialist."

An unimpressed scoff fell from Aunt Gina, and Arden's fingers curled into her clammy palms, her fingernails biting into flesh. She should have known bringing a date wouldn't be so smooth sailing. Everybody had been so enamoured with Josh. More enamoured sometimes than Arden had been.

"See what I mean, Arden? Josh is a *lawyer*," Aunt Gina replied.

"I'm well aware of my ex-husband's occupation, Aunt Gina," Arden ground out carefully. In fact, Josh's career had been one of the many things to pose a rift between them. Like Aunt Gina, Josh always seemed to look down on anybody who didn't work in a fancy office or courtroom in dull, black suits. He'd always made Arden's pottery sound more like a hobby than her livelihood, suggesting that she should go back to college and consider "her next steps." When she'd get home late from the studio, he would make a huge deal of it, claiming she didn't want to spend time with him, but when he'd get home at ten o'clock in the evening most nights still wired from the case he was working, it was his job and it was important — like hers wasn't. Like she was just biding time while he worked all day.

"I'm just saying…" Aunt Gina shrugged, chewing violently on a sprout. "You and Josh always had that spark, and he could support you financially. How much do you earn in marketing, Rosie?"

"*Gina*," her Dad interjected, shooting his sister a brusque look of disapproval. "Rosie's salary is none of your concern. Arden can support herself, and she deserves a chance to be happy with whoever it is she chooses."

Grateful, Arden glanced back at Rosie with concern. Rosie had gone quiet, her features taut and her posture locked as though she was afraid to so much as move. Guilt swirled through Arden, and she found Rosie's hand beneath the table. It was the only attempt at an apology she could manage without all eyes being drawn to them again.

She was surprised at how easily their hands kept slotting into place. Arden kept seeking Rosie, and Rosie was always waiting to be found. Rosie's palms were warm and a little bit damp. Soft. She lifted her eyes to Arden in question, and Arden stared back intently, desperate to show her how sorry she was. Nobody deserved to be treated like this, especially not when she was doing Arden a favour by being here. It was embarrassing. Awful.

Her disgust fuelled her with enough strength to speak up. "Clearly, Josh and I didn't work. It's time for me to move on. I found Rosie when I least expected, and I'd like to see where it goes. Maybe different is good for me. It *feels* good for me, anyway."

"I think it's great for you," Quinn added with a sly smirk. Arden couldn't quite decipher what it meant — but then, these days, there wasn't much she did understand about her sister.

"Me too!" Aunt Gina's middle child, Presley, piped up.

"Me three," Murray agreed, his eyes flitting to Arden above the poinsettia centrepiece. "Don't get me wrong, Josh is a good friend, but... he didn't give you the happiness you deserve. Anybody who knows you could see that."

"Rosie seems like just the girl who could." Her dad tipped his glass towards Rosie, a smile blossoming across his face. "To Rosie."

"Oh, no —" Rosie began to protest, but it was too late. Quinn was already raising her own glass — she had at least stopped drinking out of the bottle — to toast to Rosie too. Rosie's face flushed with as much vibrancy as the flowers in front of her.

Arden squeezed Rosie's hand again before lifting her own glass. "To finding something new and different," she said in an attempt to save Rosie from further embarrassment.

Still, she locked eyes with her as she said it. Their relationship might not have been real, but... there was something floating between them. Something that had been there the moment Rosie had sat opposite Arden in the bakery. Rosie was different and she was new, and it was exhilarating to learn more about her in the two days they'd spent together. Arden had found out this morning that Rosie whistled along to the radio with eerily perfect melodies, and last week, she'd discovered that Rosie licked the icing off her cupcakes before eating the cake itself. She'd seen Rosie blot her lipstick carefully to even it out rather than smacking her lips together as most people would, and she'd noticed that she had a crescent-shaped miniature scar just under her left eye.

And she'd found that when she held Rosie's hand, Rosie relaxed and would tap a rhythm on Arden's knuckles. It was as though Rosie was playing a silent song on Arden's skin, a song Arden wanted to keep listening to.

So no. Maybe the relationship wasn't real, but that didn't mean Arden didn't want to see Rosie again after today. It didn't mean it was all a lie.

"Speaking of new and different," her dad continued, dabbing the corners of his mouth with his napkin. "It's Murray's birthday next weekend, and since it's the big five-o, I planned something a little different."

"A little dangerous," Murray added with the roll of his eyes.

"God, not skydiving," Quinn said.

"*Definitely* not," Murray replied.

"Strip club?" Leo chimed in hopefully.

Arden really did despise him.

Murray's mom almost choked on her teeth in shock, leaving Murray to pat her on the back.

"Er, not quite, Leo... No, we booked a weekend cabin in an adventure park. Zip lines, kayaking, tree-climbing... all that good stuff." Her dad beamed with pride, but nobody else seemed to share the excitement.

Especially not Arden. Family holidays usually ended in disaster when they were all firmly on the ground, never mind when they were hooked to a harness twenty feet in the air or paddling down a river in a flimsy boat. And it was *winter*. "Won't it be cold?"

Her dad shrugged. "I've heard that you can buy these things called coats."

Murray only batted his hand dismissively. "You don't have to come if you don't want to, Ard. We'll celebrate when I'm back. Besides, I invited my office, so... He Who Shall Not Be Named might make an appearance."

"*Oooh*, then count me in!" Aunt Gina grinned. Arden was beginning to suspect that she had a little bit of a crush on Josh.

"Quinn?" Dad asked. "You in?"

Quinn guzzled the last of her drink and ruffled Leo's hair. "What the hell. Why not? How about you, Leo?"

"Damn," Leo replied, voice monotone. "I have plans. Maybe next time."

Arden raised an eyebrow. She just hoped there would be no alcohol on this trip. Quinn on an adventure holiday sounded like a recipe for disaster. At least Leo wouldn't be there to make things worse.

"Arden?"

Nervously, Arden twirled the stem of her own glass as all eyes fell to her. Murray was a good step-dad and his birthday was important to her... but seeing Josh for the first time since the divorce? Everybody would be talking about it. She wouldn't be able to hide, either, if they were sharing a cabin.

"Hey, you should come too, Rosie!" Quinn suggested.

If the table wasn't so large, Arden would have kicked Quinn right in the shin.

Rosie, thank heavens, shook her head immediately. "No, no, I'm not very coordinated and I don't do heights. Thank you, though."

"Oh, but it would be fun!" Quinn pouted, as immature as ever. "Arden, tell your girlfriend she has to come! It'll be your first holiday as a couple!"

Had last week's events completely wiped themselves from Quinn's memory? Had she already forgotten that Rosie and Arden weren't *actually* dating? Arden's brows drew together, half in confusion and half in disapproval. "I think it's a little early for that."

"Regardless, we would all love to have you both there," their dad said, ever the mediator. "Besides, Arden, haven't you always wanted to get out of your comfort zone a little bit? You were talking about those helicopter rides just last week."

A helicopter ride was a little bit different than soaring through a forest on a wire, but Arden didn't bother to say so. She worried at her lip, glancing at Rosie. She supposed the adventure park *would* be fun, and it *was* Murray's birthday... but the more they weaved this web of lies, the harder it would be to put a stop to it. She couldn't drag Rosie to another family event. It wouldn't be fair.

Or at least, Arden didn't think it would until Rosie confessed, "I *have* always wanted to do an adventure park. All of my friends went on a school trip to one in primary school, but I ended up getting my tonsils out that week so I couldn't go. But — "

"Then it's settled!" Murray clapped his hands with finality, and Arden knew that was it. There was no getting out of it now. "We're all going. Wonderful."

"Fabulous," Gina said.

Quinn's eyes danced with mischief as she

looked at Arden and Rosie. "Magnificent."

"Splendid," Rosie contributed for good measure.

Arden had nothing further to add — nothing, at least, but a grimace of dread. Her ex-husband and the girl she was pretending to date. Two worlds colliding...

Splendid wasn't quite the word Arden would have chosen.

∞∞∞

"I have a confession to make." Rosie winced and pressed her forehead against the window, watching the first dregs of snow flutter onto the glass. The night was pitch-black and damp enough that with any luck, it wouldn't stick. Rosie didn't feel like trudging through grey sludge on her way to work tomorrow, though she supposed it would be better than the number of times she'd risked a black ice-related injury in New York's freezing conditions. And she thought that British weather was bad...

Arden's only response was a questioning hum as she flicked on the indicator. She'd grown almost unreachable as she drove, perhaps because of the dark, and her tongue kept poking out in concentration. It was annoyingly sweet and not something Rosie wanted to notice.

"I'm afraid of heights," Rosie went on. "Like,

heart palpitations, sweaty armpits, jelly legs, snot-running-down-my-face scared. I won't be able to do the zip wire thingy."

Golden streetlights danced across Arden's features, highlighting her furrowed brows. "You really, really don't have to go next weekend. I wouldn't expect you to. Christmas was the deal — and you saved me a world of fatherly concern, by the way. Thank you."

"I don't mind. I had a good time tonight," Rosie said quickly, her heart fluttering, tugging, reaching out as though it was made of two splayed hands far greedier than her own. She'd enjoyed tonight. She'd enjoyed being around people who weren't co-workers with nine a.m. coffee breath or commuters who looked like they were about to murder her when she sat beside them on public transport. The prospect of going home to her dark, empty flat, where she still hadn't unpacked half of her boxes…

She wasn't adjusting to New York life well, but tonight, she had. Just for a moment, she'd been okay. Arden had held her hand, and she hadn't felt alone. Her family had smiled at her like maybe she mattered, like maybe she was good and wanted, and she didn't want any of it to just fall away when the flashing neon green analogue clock on the dashboard struck midnight.

"Maybe that's against the fake-dating rules…" she considered, suddenly bashful at her own vulnerability.

"We didn't set any rules." The corner of Arden's lip twitched with the ghost of a smile. "And I had a good time, too. Maybe... Maybe it doesn't *all* have to be fake. We could be friends, at least. I mean, there's no reason not to be. And I'd be more than happy to return the favour if you ever needed a date of your own for whatever reason."

Rosie wasn't invited to anything that required a date, and nobody in the city cared one bit about her non-existent love life, but the sentiment left her warm and tingly all the same. It was nice having a friend — someone she connected with and someone who seemed to like her company. "I'd like to be friends."

"Good. Me too."

At ease, Rosie sank further into her seat, the silhouettes of towering architecture growing closer by the minute. "Are you sure you want me there, though, what with your ex-husband going too? I wouldn't want to intrude or complicate things."

"There's nothing to complicate. Josh and I have been divorced for over a year. If anything, you'd be doing me a favour. He might stay away if he thinks I'm with someone." Arden's words were light, neutral, and Rosie frowned. A broken marriage was *never* that simple, was it?

She found evidence it wasn't in Arden's clenched jaw and her tight knuckles on the steering wheel. Rosie wished she could ask more, but she knew not to pry. They didn't know each other well enough for that. Maybe they could get to know one another, though, if Rosie managed to make it through the upcoming trip without spiralling into a panic attack if they made her climb or swing from anything above five feet from the ground. That would probably be a dealbreaker.

"I can lay it on thick if you want," Rosie suggested anyway, and then playfully ran her hand up Arden's thigh, following the pleats in her tailored trousers. "It might make him jealous." The pitch of her voice rose as she mimicked, "Oh, Arden, aren't you glad you divorced that boring lawyer and found me instead? Mwah." She blew a kiss Arden's way for good measure.

Arden laughed — a real, hoarse laugh that rolled straight from her belly. It was the first time Rosie had heard it, and she wanted to again. She wanted to tug a thousand more of those laughs from Arden. But she was suddenly very aware of the warmth of Arden's thigh through her trousers, and she pulled away, hoping she hadn't overstepped. She'd always been scolded for being a tactile person, always hugging and playing with people's hair or linking arms in the school yard.

"Thank you, Rosie," Arden said after a moment, tearing her eyes off the road to glance at her. "For coming tonight, I mean. I'm really sorry about the way Aunt Gina was, comparing you to Josh like that. I didn't know she was so attached to my ex-husband."

Rosie batted Arden's apology away. Aunt

Gina's barbed words had been uncomfortable only because Rosie couldn't imagine how they must have made Arden feel. She was just trying to move on, but her aunt seemed to want to tug her back and keep her firmly where she was — in the past. "I got your dad's approval. That's all that matters, isn't it?"

"Dad loved you. He'll be heartbroken if..." Arden's teeth trapped her bottom lip quickly, and with it, whatever Arden was about to say. She amended quickly, "If you would have said no to the trip."

"I like your sister, by the way. She's funny. I see where she gets her Don't Be a Stranger username from." After dinner, Quinn had promptly pulled out the tequila. Arden had practically dragged Rosie out of the house before things got messy. For siblings, they were so different. Arden was composed, polite, and sensible. Quinn was the polar opposite: raucous, teasing, and loud. But Rosie suspected there was more to it. The way her boyfriend had clung onto her, talked over her, made fun of her all night... Rosie had been in a relationship like that before, and it had left her feeling broken and worthless in the end. She hoped Leo wouldn't dull Quinn's sparkling spirit.

"She's..." Arden let out a ragged breath and scraped her hair from her eyes. "She's something."

The way her words wobbled just slightly...

"You're worried about her," Rosie deduced.

Surprise crossed Arden's features, hand in hand with the glow of a green traffic light. "Yeah, I am. She's always been reckless and obsessed with partying, but her boyfriend..."

"Bit of a wanker, isn't he? Pardon my French."

Arden chuffed. "That's putting it nicely, yeah. I need to talk to her about him."

"You do," Rosie agreed. "It isn't my place but... People like that try to snuff out our light. It starts out little, but it doesn't always end that way. Quinn deserves better."

"I know. I just don't know how to make her see that." Her eyes turned glassy, and sympathy tightened like a fist in Rosie's chest. "You dated someone like Leo?"

"Well, the situation was different, but I've been treated like Quinn was. I've been controlled and manipulated and belittled. I wouldn't wish it upon anyone else."

Arden looked at Rosie again, their eyes locking. And then her hand reached across the car to find Rosie's, just as it had earlier, and it was becoming too easy, too natural, for them to touch and talk and laugh. Rosie didn't know how or why. It had never been this easy before, with anyone. Maybe because they weren't really dating. Maybe because there was no pressure to be anything, and when there was, they could hide behind the guise of their act — blame it on that even when nobody else was watching them, like when Arden had held

Rosie's hand under the table at dinner.

"I'm sorry," Arden whispered. "People are just… shitty."

"Not all of them," Rosie replied. *Not you.*

Arden smiled, the shadows of the car sinking into the dimple of her chin and the valley of her Cupid's bow as though they wanted to be close to her too. Rosie tried not to look between the two, at her plump, pink lips, and wonder what they would feel like on her skin. Instead, she glanced back out the window and savoured the peaceful tranquility that followed, the car's engine lulling her into a sense of comfort she hadn't yet felt before so far from home.

Things were looking up.

Seven

*@ChefA: Is it frowned upon to ask your sister's
midwife on a date an hour after the birth? Asking
for a friend who is definitely not me.*

Rosie had spent most of the morning dozing at her desk. Her snooze was quickly relocated to a conference table in the meeting room at eleven a.m. when her boss, Ning, called everyone in. Nobody looked particularly happy about it either. Rosie stared around a sea of wan, exhausted faces. Shaheen, the head of human resources, still sported a smattering of green glitter across her cheeks, claiming that her daughter had gotten new face paints for Christmas and her first use of them had been transforming her mother into Shrek. Wade sported black-tinted Ray-Bans, claiming to have a splitting headache brought on by eye strain. Since Rosie had received a string of drunken Snapchats last night from him, she suspected that the ailment had more to do with a well-deserved hangover. And Dana, the tech advisor, slept with her mouth agape, dribble trickling down her chin and her snores a soft soundtrack to Caroline's presentation. It hitched as Caroline pointedly raised her voice in the middle of a sentence, causing Dana to sit up, alert, in her chair and wipe away the saliva with her sleeve.

It was rare that anybody actually saw Caroline in the flesh. She had been a faceless shadow looming over Rosie for the first two months of her employment. Since Postcard Development owned and developed four other social media apps and counting, their head of Don't Be a Stranger's department usually took the reins. Rosie wasn't sure why today was any different. It was Boxing Day, for starters, which meant that everybody was miserable, drained, and sick of the cold weather or else hadn't shown up at all. Besides, Caroline didn't really seem to be saying anything of importance. It was all statistics and surveys, things Rosie didn't need to understand to do her job.

She was glad when Caroline flicked to the final slide and concluded her long and tedious speech. Everybody made to leave, as desperate for freedom as high school students deafened by the three o'clock school bell, but Caroline's clipped words stopped them.

"Sit down, please. I have one final question for you all before you go."

Rosie sighed and slumped back down again, clicking the lid of her pen impatiently.

"As most of you know, we have our first mixer event coming up in January for users of Don't Be a Stranger. It's a chance for real-life interactions, where people have the option of breaking their anonymity to meet people they might have communicated with on the app, or otherwise engage in our blind dating activities. The problem is that we also want to draw in new people unfamiliar with our brand, and to do that, we need some success stories to share."

"We can certainly search for some within the app," Ning offered, "though I'm not sure how willing people would be to lose their anonymity. The appeal of Don't Be a Stranger is that most people are... strangers. It's a simple social media app that allows people to post and interact however they wish as long as it adheres to the rules."

"Well, that's a decent idea, but I was wondering if perhaps anybody in this room has used the app or knows of someone who has." Caroline smoothed down her blazer, her dark eyes scouring across each of them in turn. Rosie's pulse quickened as though her recent experience with Don't Be a Stranger was stained on her skin for everyone to see and at any moment, she'd be found out. But Caroline's gaze slid over her on its journey around the room.

She sniffed, resting her hand on the table as though they were all in for a scolding. "Come on, people. We need to get more hands-on in our approach here. Not one person here has actually *used* the app?"

"Rosie has! I saw her using it this morning!"

It was Wade who volunteered the information from beside her, and just for good measure, raised his hand and pointed at her head. Rosie grimaced and tried to yank Wade's arm down, but he was twice her size and must have had the muscles of a personal trainer hidden beneath his shirt.

"Rosie?" Caroline raised an eyebrow, freezing Rosie beneath her icy focus. "Do you use Don't Be a Stranger?"

"Er…" Rosie shifted. She could lie. But then what if Caroline found out? She could be fired, and then what? She'd left everything behind for this job. She'd *prayed* for this job. She *liked* this job. She didn't want to lose it. "I scroll through it occasionally."

"And has it led to anything? A date, a relationship, even a friendship, perhaps? Anything that we can showcase at our mixer?"

No, was the instinctive answer, and she opened her mouth to say so when Caroline continued: "It would certainly put you in with the chance of a promotion if you *did* give us the chance to offer up a positive story. Imagine how many people's hope would be rekindled in online dating if we gave them a personal, magical fairytale of love firsthand. I must admit, the number of new users signing up has dwindled of late. This would get us back on track." She narrowed her eyes as though willing Rosie to give her the answer she wanted to hear. Rosie had a feeling that Caroline wouldn't accept anything less now. She also had a feeling that Caroline wasn't looking for the truth, as long as the story they came up with could be used to promote the app.

And then Arden's words from last night echoed in her mind, "*And I'd be more than happy to return the favour if you ever needed a date of your own for whatever reason.*" Rosie hadn't thought she'd ever take Arden up on such an offer, but now… She supposed it was only fair. Arden had gotten her use out of Rosie, even more so when they went on the trip next weekend. Why couldn't Rosie take advantage of their agreement too? It could get her a promotion. A higher salary. That meant a less crummy apartment, maybe even in a safer part of Manhattan.

"I've been on a few dates with someone I met on the app," she admitted finally, chewing on her bottom lip. "It's early days, though."

Half of her co-workers — the ones still awake at least — let out an "*aww*," and Rosie's cheeks blazed with fire.

"Tell us all about it," Caroline urged, perching on the table now and crossing her arms over her chest. "How did it come about?"

"Well…" Rosie couldn't lie to save her life, and even if she wanted to, if they dug for Quinn's original post, they'd know it was all fake. The only reason she managed to get this far was because she and Arden had found a way to stir in sprinkles of truths within their pretence. She tried to do that now. "A user made a post looking for a fake date for Christmas because their family was worried that they weren't dating anyone. I happened to be free, so… I replied. We met up and got on better than expected, and the rest is history, I suppose."

"So you're seeing each other again soon?"

Rosie nodded. "Yep."

"Good. Bring them to the mixer. I can see it now." Caroline wafted her hands about in front of her as though mimicking a photograph frame. "Rosie Gladwell, our very own spokesperson for Don't Be a Stranger, standing on stage and telling us all about her wonderful love story that started out with just a post and a pretence. *Ooh*, and we can have screen grabs of the messages projected on a huge screen behind you! It'll be magnificent!"

"Oh, no, I don't —" Rosie attempted to protest, but Caroline's eager words interrupted her.

"Yes, then it's sorted. Rosie, I'm very impressed with the dedication you've shown to your department. Be sure to email over your Don't Be a Stranger username to Dana. I expect to see everybody else in this room at the mixer, too, unless you have a valid reason to miss such an important event. I would encourage *all* of you to become more familiar with the app like Rosie has. Rosie's passion has earned her both a real love story and a spotlight here at the company. Perhaps her success may provide you all with more incentive to approach your work with the same investment."

Caroline marched out of the meeting room with her upturned nose dragging through the air like a shark fin through grey sea. As the door slammed shut, everybody's eyes turned to Rosie. She wanted to disappear and kicked her legs out beneath the table to sink further down in her chair.

Wade patted her shoulder, a proud smile on his chiselled face. "Congrats, Rosie! You're the boss's new favourite gal!"

Rosie shot him a venom-filled glower. "Thanks a lot, Wade. I didn't know you'd been *spying* on me."

Wade only rolled his eyes and rose from his chair, slinging his leather satchel across his shoulder. "You're welcome. I was going to ask if you wanted to grab lunch together, but…"

Rosie's stomach grumbled, and she sighed. She was starving, and lunch with Wade was about the only chance she got to be social at work. Nobody else paid her much attention, and she found it difficult to make friends in an office where most people already knew one another. She felt like an intruder around them all.

"Where?" Rosie asked, defeated.

"Angelo's?"

Her tongue tingled with hunger at the

thought of pizza. "Fine. You're forgiven. But you're paying."

Wade smirked. "Deal."

Eight

@GamerGuy00: My mom says I spend too much time playing Skyrim and it's time I found myself a girlfriend. I think she's right about the girlfriend thing, so this is me beginning my search. I am looking for a fellow Dragonborn to accompany me on dangerous quests and love me even when I accidentally become a vampire. Must be handy with a sword and have potions of health to hand. Any takers?

Arden didn't know what she'd been thinking, agreeing to go on a trip with her pretend girlfriend and her ex-husband. The nerves had been rattling through her all morning as she drove to New Jersey with Rosie in the passenger seat. She tapped the steering wheel restlessly to the beat of a blaring pop song on the radio, trying not to think about all the ways in which this could go horribly wrong.

It wasn't that she and Josh had ended on bad terms — but maybe that was the problem. What if he still had feelings for her? What if *she* still had feelings for *him*? Or what if he hated her for the divorce? What if Rosie was dragged into it? He could be jealous. She knew that about him already. Rosie didn't deserve to be subjected to Arden's problems, and she certainly didn't deserve to have to pretend to be Arden's date for her sake. It was all a big, big mess, and Arden was terrified.

"Are you okay?" Rosie questioned as signs for the adventure park finally began to approach. They had turned off the highway and onto a winding, narrow lane of skeletal trees and lifeless shrubbery, all layered by a thick frost that only proved winter was not the time to be outdoorsy. But Murray had never liked to follow rules. He usually ordered chocolate fudge cake for dinner.

"Uh-huh," Arden replied. It was unconvincing even to her own ears.

"Are you sure?" Rosie's brows furrowed in Arden's periphery. "It's okay to be nervous, you know. I would be."

"It's just weird. All of this is weird, isn't it?"

She shrugged. "It doesn't have to be. I mean, it was weird at first but… I like you, Arden. As a friend, I mean. Not…" She trailed off, sighing as though grappling for the words. "I just mean that there are worse people in the world to pretend to date. I like spending time with you, so maybe we can just be us, be friends, and not care about what everyone else thinks we are."

"It feels like a lie," Arden admitted quietly, guiltily. "I'm really glad that my family likes you, but I'm also worried they like you *too* much. At what point does it get out of hand? When do we put a stop to it?"

"Do you want to set a date? Like, a date that we fake breakup?"

God, no, Arden didn't want that. She didn't want to stop seeing Rosie just because they'd said they should when they were feeling guilty and confused. She just... She didn't know when they'd gotten here. And she didn't know when she'd started enjoying it so much. It wasn't like she wanted to *actually* date Rosie. She wasn't ready for that, and they were still practically strangers, no matter how much it felt otherwise. But this could get complicated, and Arden didn't know how to handle it.

It was Quinn's fault for posting that damn ad in the first place.

"No, I don't want to plan a fake breakup." Her words softened with sincerity as her fingers relaxed against the steering wheel. "You're right. I'm being silly. We get on well and us being together is beneficial for both of us, so what does it matter what everyone else expects?"

"Exactly." Rosie nodded, though her voice seemed to crack just slightly as she peered out of the window and repeated, "Beneficial."

"We should probably keep PDA to a minimum when Josh is around this weekend, though," Arden continued. "Out of respect for him, I mean. I don't know how he'll take me seeing someone new."

"I get that. Actually, I've been meaning to —" Rosie stuttered over her words as they rolled into the adventure park, looking up through her eyelashes at the towering trees and the activities stationed around them in the air. "Oh, good gravy. I'm going to die."

Arden couldn't find the zip line Murray had planned for them, though littered around the main leisure centre, she saw plenty of people in winter workout gear climbing trees and ladders, hiking across wooden bridges that didn't seem so sturdy, and leaping from platforms to swing from dangling hoops and rope.

It definitely wasn't the place for somebody afraid of heights.

"You don't have to do anything you don't want to," Arden reminded gently as she turned into a parking spot. Behind the leisure centre, she could make out a cluster of cabins. Josh might already be in one of them.

Rosie's throat bobbed with a swallow. Her hazel eyes darkened to the same shade as the evergreen trees outside, and she remained fixed on one spot in the cloudy grey sky.

The whirring engine ebbed, leaving them blanketed in silence. Clearing her throat, Arden unfastened her seatbelt — and when Rosie still remained frozen minutes later, did the same for her too.

"Rosie," she breathed, trying to pull her back to the car, to the present. "You'll be fine, promise.

You really don't have to do the height stuff."

"We can't just sit everything out all weekend because I'm a bit scared, can we?" Rosie seemed to break out of her trance, pasting on a false smile. "No, we can't. Let's do this. It's only heights and ex-husbands, isn't it? How bad can it be?"

It could have been terrible, but Arden didn't think it'd be helpful to say so. So, with a final, reassuring squeeze of Rosie's shoulder, she got out of the car and prepared herself to face a weekend of chaos.

∞ ∞ ∞

Despite Arden's request of no PDA, she and Rosie walked into the cabin hand in hand. Rosie's blood hummed with nerves, but she eased when she was greeted by Arden's dad and Murray, and then Quinn afterwards, all of them chorusing "Happy New Year!" to one another. A glass of whiskey was instantly thrust into Rosie's hands by the latter, and she didn't hesitate before gulping it down. She would need it to get through the weekend.

Quinn refilled the glass, and then Arden chugged her own drink, earning her a cheer. Murray ushered them into the kitchen to introduce Rosie to the family she hadn't met yet — his brother, Jackson, and his wife, Moira — and his colleagues. She wondered which one of the charming, well-dressed lawyers was Arden's ex, if any, and didn't have to wait long to find out.

A sandy-haired man emerged from the group, tipping his glass toward them. "Aren't you going to introduce me, Murray?"

Arden's warm presence turned to cool ice against Rosie's back. "Josh." Her voice was breathy, an attempt at nonchalance that Rosie saw straight through.

"Arden." Josh's light eyes twinkled with familiarity, and something else, something that Rosie read as flirtatiousness. "And you must be Rosie, Arden's..."

"Girlfriend." Rosie didn't know why she was so quick to say it. She offered Josh a polite nod, trying not to notice how perfectly handsome he was: the sort of man who was better suited to play a rom-com hero. He had chiselled cheeks and a neatly-trimmed golden stubble, broad shoulders, and perfect teeth. Rosie had none of these attributes, and she felt... icky to think that to everyone here, she was probably the ditzy, frumpy girl who had followed the successful, attractive lawyer in Arden's recent history. The rebound.

"Of course. It's a pleasure to meet you. And it's good to see you, Ard."

Ard. A pang of something foul shot through Rosie. She was glad when, uncomfortably, Murray offered to show them to their room. She didn't know if Arden would follow — could only hope she would — but when they reached the foot of the stairs, Rosie found her hovering behind them with a meek smile. Murray offered to carry their bags, and then they were traipsing up the carpeted steps together, onto an open landing that looked down onto the ground floor. There, Rosie caught Josh's glance shifting up, seeking Arden. She pretended not to notice the second jolt of jealousy in as many minutes turning her blood hot.

"Here it is. We saved one of the best rooms for you two. Not too shabby, is it?" Murray opened the door to the third room on the right. "Are you okay, sweetheart?" he asked Arden.

"Why wouldn't I be?" Arden reassured, placing a kiss on her step-father's cheek before stepping into the bedroom. Rosie followed hesitantly, her heart slamming against her ribs when she saw the double bed neatly made with a green plaid quilt and a heap of fluffy cushions. She hadn't even thought about sleeping arrangements, too lost in the ex-boyfriend and fake-dating of it all. She supposed it could have been worse: they could have been in a tent like the campers she'd seen lugging about their things outside.

"We're heading out to the zip line in an hour. Wrap up warm, kids." Murray placed their luggage on a rustic brown armchair, rubbed his hands together, and then wandered off, leaving them alone.

"So..." Rosie stepped further into the room, her boots hitting the soft rug beneath the bed. "You didn't mention that your ex is ridiculously good-looking. I would have made more effort with my makeup if I'd known."

Arden snorted, though Rosie wasn't joking. She checked her hair in the full-length mirror propped by the dresser and found it as unruly as ever. She had long since stopped trying to tame it, especially when chopping most of it off had done nothing to help. Josh's had been perfectly slicked back, not a strand out of place.

Ugh. Her stomach twisted with insecurity, shame, dread — and, fine, perhaps a little bit of envy. Not that she wanted to be a fancy lawyer with a nice jawline. She liked the way she looked — cellulite and stomach rolls and gapped smile and all — but did Arden?

Arden appeared in the mirror behind Rosie, dragging her away. "Please don't do that. You always look beautiful."

Rosie didn't know how to respond to a compliment like that, though it sent her heart swimming into her stomach. "How do you feel? Are you... regretting this? Did you get the feels?"

Arden wrinkled her nose. "The feels?"

"You know." Rosie sunk down onto the thick mattress. "When you see an ex again for the first time in ages and you get the feels all over again. Your belly goes *whoosh* and your heart flops about in your chest like a dying fish and —"

"Your experiences of feelings are not universal, I don't think." The corner of Arden's mouth tugged with a smirk as she sat beside Rosie.

Her perfume wafted around them, sweet and floral and reminding Rosie of spring. "No, I didn't get the feels. No dying fish here. And I don't regret this. I'm glad you're here with me."

"Good because I have a favour to ask." Rosie swiped her clammy palms across her thermal leggings, following the advice of a framed affirmation reading: *If not now, when?* She'd tried earlier, but seeing the activity platforms stationed in intimidatingly tall trees had distracted her from anything else.

"I think I owe you more than a few already. Shoot."

"So... " She blew her sweaty fringe from her eyes, unsure why she was so nervous. If she could meet a stranger in a bakery and offer to pretend to be their girlfriend for Christmas, she could ask for the same in return for the sake of a work promotion, couldn't she? "I had a work meeting last week. We're holding a mixer event thing for users of Don't Be a Stranger, and my boss asked for success stories to promote the app. Thing is, my annoying co-worker dropped me right in it and told everyone I've been using it, so my boss asked me to come to the mixer... with you... to promote it. *We found love and so can you, blah, blah, blah.*"

Arden raised a brow. "Isn't that false advertising?"

Rosie hadn't even thought of that. She'd been more concerned about asking Arden on a date and the pressure Caroline had been putting on

Rosie since agreeing to go. She would have to write a speech, to be said in front of everyone. It was going to be traumatising, to say the least. And then there were all the poor people who would believe her when she told them about finding love on the app. People who would hold out hope because Rosie told them to, even though it was a lie.

"You're right. It's really bad. Maybe I can fake a stomach bug or something on the night and just... not go." And then maybe she would be fired the following day for backing out on the one task Caroline expected of her.

"No, we should go. It's the least I can do. Besides, we might not be a real success story, but there *have* been some... like the couple we saw in Washington Square Park. It's not like it would *all* be a lie just to promote the app."

"We would probably have to lay it on thick," Rosie contemplated. "Thicker than we have already. Like, peanut butter-thick. This is about people having faith in love and the app. Well, actually it's about getting more people to sign up but... you know."

"Do you have faith?" Arden asked.

Rosie faltered, both from the question and the way Arden was looking at her — her eyes gleaming with curiosity and her lips curling into a soft smile. The low mid-afternoon light haloed her so that it was impossible to tell where the sun ended and Arden's golden hair began. Rosie didn't always feel like she was here, tethered to the Earth like everyone else. She often felt as though she was floating, drifting, her mind in a million places at once and her presence, her physical entity, wasn't something she necessarily considered except when she was finding a way to embarrass herself. But with Arden looking at her like that… it anchored her for a moment. Rosie was real again and here, grounded, because Arden was *seeing* her.

It dragged the truth from her. "I've always had faith. It's why I go on the app. I see so many people connecting. Not to sound like Hugh Grant from *Love Actually*, but love *is* everywhere, and the app helps me notice it."

"Then it's not a lie," Arden murmured. "And we'll lay it on thick… as peanut butter."

It was all Rosie could have hoped for. "Thank you, Arden. It means a lot."

"Besides, we did find *something* on the app, didn't we?" Arden placed her hand on Rosie's thigh and squeezed. "I don't know what it is, but I know I like spending time with you… that's something."

Rosie was speechless, a fire scorching the pit of her stomach. She could do nothing but nod and try to remember how to breathe as Arden stood and began to unpack.

If her body kept responding to Arden this way, maybe laying it on thick at the mixer would be easier than expected.

∞ ∞ ∞

"Where's your sister, Ard? Is she not joining us?" Josh asked as Arden and Rosie crunched their way to the zip line's meeting point. A few of Murray's colleagues had begun without him, already climbing the wooden rungs nailed to a thick tree trunk to get to the top. The platform looked out onto a murky lake. It might have served as a soft landing if it all went wrong had it not been iced over by the unforgiving winter. Arden tried not to focus on it as her dad and Murray approached behind, chatting happily.

She skimmed past them, expecting to find Quinn trailing them, but only Aunt Gina and her eldest son followed.

"I guess she found something better to do." Or just a bar somewhere. Arden hadn't had a chance to speak to her properly about Leo still, and a kernel of guilt weighed in her stomach at the fact. Once, she'd spent day and night fretting over Quinn and her bad decisions, just as she had with her mom, but recently… she was done with it. She would always worry and would always care, but she couldn't fix people who seemed to enjoy being broken. She was sick of always feeling like it was her responsibility. Quinn had made so many choices that had led her here, and how could Arden change that now?

"Who's next?" one of the adventure park guides called from the foot of the tree, extending a harness tucked inside an unflattering yellow helmet.

Murray and her dad were the first to volunteer themselves, helping each other into their gear. It left an awkward silence soon filled by Aunt Gina.

"Hello, Joshua. You're looking very well these days. Have you been working out?"

Arden wanted to gag. Instead, she only pursed her lips and watched Josh scratch the back of his neck uncomfortably. "A little. Thanks, Aunt Gina."

"I was just saying to Arden last week how much I loved you two together." She fluffed her hair up, damn near shoving Rosie out of the way to get closer to Josh. "Out of all the people she's dated, you're my favourite."

Anger spiked through Arden. It was one thing to try to belittle Rosie at the dinner table, but it was another to do it in front of Arden's ex-husband. Gritting her teeth, she laced Rosie's hand through hers, catching Rosie's look of surprise from the corner of her eye. "Well, he's a free man now, Aunt Gina, if you want to take a crack at him. Lucky you. And lucky me for finding Rosie. Seems like everything turned out perfectly."

Josh's brows knitted together, his eyes piercing. Arden had forgotten just how sharp, dangerous, they could be. Where hers were deep cobalt, his were like Quinn's — pale, near translucent, as biting as the icy lake surrounding them. "How long have the two of you been dating?"

"Two months," Arden answered.

He seemed to relax, a muscle in his jaw quivering as though with restrained amusement. "Not long, then. Still in your honeymoon period?"

Arden's upper lip curled apprehensively. She didn't like the way he seemed to subtly sneer at the question, as though implying their relationship didn't matter because they hadn't been together very long. Not that it was real, but... still. He had no right. "You proposed to me after three months, so I guess time doesn't mean much."

"You said yes." His eyes danced with conceit.

"And how long did it take for you to divorce?" Rosie asked. Her eyes widened with innocence, but her words had a sharp thorn hidden beneath the silk petals of her voice — one that Arden relished in, just to watch Josh's smirk falter. She hadn't meant for it to come to this, but she couldn't stand by and let Aunt Gina and Josh patronise her for moving on. Especially not when they used Rosie as a way of doing it.

"Next!" The guide called. Aunt Gina stepped back, returning to her place in the queue behind Arden.

With a crooked smirk, Josh motioned ahead of him. "Ladies first."

Arden glanced at Rosie in question.

"I'll wait down here," said Rosie.

"Not a fan of heights?" There it was again, that lazy, teasing tone Josh had used when Arden had talked to... well, anyone. He was an asshole when he was jealous, and Arden had always despised that about him. For an attractive, wealthy, successful man, he seemed to be threatened by an awful lot of people.

"Not really, no."

"Come on, don't be a spoilsport. You'll be attached to a harness. What's the worst that can happen?"

Another attribute Arden had forgotten she'd hated about her ex-husband: his need to control, to convince people to do the things he wanted. It was helpful in a courtroom when persuading a jury of his client's innocence but irritating for the people around him.

"Isn't it a little boring to come to an adventure park and stand on your own?" Aunt Gina piped up.

"You know what? We'll meet you across the lake." Arden pulled Rosie out of the group, feeling suddenly claustrophobic. She could only imagine how Rosie felt.

"You should conquer your fears, Rosie!" Josh called. "Besides, Arden loves the zip line."

And then Arden wasn't pulling her away anymore. Rosie stopped and tugged her back, her features set into fine lines of determination as she looked back at Josh.

"Rosie," Arden whispered. "You don't have to do this. They're acting like children."

"But you shouldn't have to miss out because of me."

"I'm not missing out. I don't give a shit about the zip line." It wasn't a lie. She did love putting herself out there, participating, especially where adrenaline was involved, but she didn't have anything to prove to Josh and neither did Rosie. Arden hated him — for the first time in her life, she hated him — for making Rosie feel as though she did.

The guide huffed. "Is anyone going up, or are we going to stand here all day?"

Only a beat passed before Rosie said, "I will." Her voice shook, and it caused Arden's stomach to drop.

"Rosie —"

But it was too late. Rosie was walking slowly over to the guide. Arden followed, smoothing her features into cold stone as she glanced at Aunt Gina and Josh in turn. Josh only shrugged as though he hadn't played any part in this.

"Step into the harness," the guide ordered, holding out the harness for Rosie. She did as asked, but Arden didn't miss the tremble in her knees and hands as she was buckled up. It was Arden's turn afterwards, but she barely noticed the tightening straps around her midsection. The colour had been leached from Rosie's face, leaving her grey.

"You really, really don't have to do this,"

Arden reminded.

"I do. I need to get over this so I can go home." Rosie buckled her helmet, her hair flattening beneath the plastic.

"What do you mean?"

"I'm terrified to get back on a plane so I haven't been able to visit my family. Maybe this will help."

Arden sucked in a breath and nodded before fastening her own helmet. "Okay. Then we'll do it together."

"Actually, it's one at a time, but you can climb up together," the instructor droned, sounding bored.

Rosie didn't look back at the others as she stalked over to the tree and put her foot on the first rung. Her knuckles turned white as she clutched the higher panels of wood for support. She bowed her head before letting out a ragged breath.

Arden knew better than to try to talk her out of it again. Instead, she placed a tender hand on the small of Rosie's back. "I'm right behind you."

A nod. And then Rosie pushed off the ground, her boots bringing up mud and soggy leaves with them as she climbed. Once she was high enough, Arden followed, stopping only on the eighth rung.

"Oh, bollocks," Rosie muttered.

Arden peered up and found her head bowed, her eyes squeezed shut.

"You're okay," she soothed. "You're almost at

the top."

They were only halfway, but it wouldn't have been helpful to point it out.

A mangled choke fell from Rosie, and then she continued on up another four rungs. Now, Arden's words of comfort were true. The brisk wind clawed through Arden's hair and stung her cheeks as the falling leaves rustled off their branches above them. She could see the head of the other guide peering over the platform above them, shouting words of encouragement. She could see Rosie's face sliced apart by tears.

"We can go back down, Rosie. It's okay," Arden said.

"Come on, Rosie!" The calls came from the bottom, from Josh. "Attagirl!"

Her breaths fell from her in uneven and jagged shudders as her helmet kissed the ladder's rung as she slumped again. "Why am I doing this?"

"Because you're brave," Arden suggested.

"I'm not. I'm flipping terrified."

"But you're doing it anyway." She braved taking one hand from the ladder, placing it on the only part of Rosie she could, her calf. "We can go down if you want to, Rosie, but you're almost there. Just a few more steps."

Rosie whimpered. "It's so high."

"Only if you look down." It was shitty advice, but Arden had nothing better. She squeezed Rosie's quivering calf a final time and knew, somehow, that Rosie wouldn't ask to go down now. She'd come all this way. The fact she'd done this at all, knowing how afraid she'd be, said enough.

Sure enough, Rosie straightened and took another step.

"Good girl," Arden murmured. She had no idea if Rosie heard. Still, she continued on, swaying on the penultimate step. The guide pulled her up onto the platform, and then she was there, sitting at the top of the tree.

Arden climbed up behind her, finding Rosie slumped. Her eyes were squeezed shut, tears still slipping onto her cheeks.

"You did it." Arden swiped the damp away, her thumb tracing across galaxies of freckles. "You're at the top."

"I can't do it. I can't do the zip line," she croaked.

"That's okay. We don't have to."

She sniffled. Arden glanced behind her to find a way down that wouldn't make Rosie feel worse — but she froze when she caught Josh already hauling himself onto the platform. His features fell when he saw the state Rosie was in, sympathy and what Arden hoped was guilt swirling across his face.

As though sensing him, Rosie's eyes flew open, bloodshot and red-rimmed, and she pulled herself up slowly. Arden followed, tilting up Rosie's chin when her eyes flew to the ground below.

"Don't look down there. Look at me."

Her chin wobbled, but she kept it clamped stubbornly as she gazed at Arden. Something shifted in Arden's world then because she knew that she was currently standing in the centre of Rosie's. And maybe Rosie was the centre of hers.

"If you want my advice," the guide said, sighing, "I'd go on the zip line. It's an easier way down than climbing. Quicker, too."

"You should go, Josh," Arden ordered. He wasn't helping Rosie make her decision by being here, and Arden was sick of the weight of his presence, even if his smarmy smirk had been wiped off his lips.

He hesitated. "I can help…"

Clutching the railings of the platform, Rosie braved a step forward to look down at the ladders. Her eyes fluttered shut a moment later, and she stumbled back again. "I don't think I can climb back down. I think I'll have to do the zip line."

"Do you want to go first? Get it over with?" asked Josh.

Feebly, she nodded. "Okay."

"Let's get you fastened in, then." The guide urged her forward, and Arden led her closer to the edge, to the place Rosie was so afraid of. Josh trailed behind them, his hands hovering as though he didn't know what to do with them. It seemed he'd lost his attitude now that he was no longer on the ground.

Rosie stood stock-still as the guide clipped her harness to the line, and it left Arden holding her breath too.

"Okay. Ready to go?"

"No," Rosie admitted, but she managed a wry, if not terse, smile. Fragments of sunset bleeding through the trees dappled her in pink and amber.

"You're doing so well, Rosie," Arden reassured.

The guide told her where to put her hands and then there was nothing left to do but wait for Rosie to jump.

"Okay," she breathed. "It's fine. I'm fine. I'm only about to dangle ten feet from the floor on a thin wire."

"It's all very safe," the guide promised, though Arden caught her rolling her eyes.

"You got this," Josh added.

"Arden?" Rosie called.

"Yep?"

"Can you push me?"

Arden raised her eyebrows. "Are you sure?"

Rosie nodded frantically, and Arden steeled herself before stepping forward, past the guide. Ahead of them, the forest yawned out, daunting and endless. Beneath them, the icy, still lake waited with claws. Arden understood why Rosie was afraid but with the fear came the excitement of plunging into it all headfirst.

"Okay. Should I count you down?"

"No," Rosie said. "Just do it." And then she started humming — the first notes of what sounded like "Rocket Man" by Elton John.

"What are you doing?"

"I'm trying to find my happy place." And then, louder, the first verse of what was most definitely "Rocket Man." Then she shouted, "Just bloody well do it, Arden!"

Arden waited until Rosie reached the chorus to make her move, nudging Rosie forward. Her shriek rent through the birdsong and billowing wind, and her figure shrank as she fell away from Arden, from the world.

With a swell of pride cresting in her chest, Arden clapped. So did Josh. So did the guide.

Of course, Rosie was too busy screaming to hear them.

Nine

*@KeepingupwithKyle: My brother forced me to come
to an adventure park and I swear I just saw a girl get
pushed off a zip line. Is that even legal? I'm concerned.
Do I report it? Pretty sure she screamed "fuck it, man" on
the way down. This place is freaky. I wanna go home.*

"Have you forgiven me yet?" Arden collapsed onto the cabin's damp porch steps beside Rosie, offering out a steaming mug of what Rosie hoped was an Irish coffee. She still hadn't recovered from the trauma of the zip line, and the shock made her bones jitter like wind chimes in a hurricane.

But she'd done it. That had to have counted for something, didn't it? It felt like it did. Not that she wished to do it again any time soon, but maybe it was a step in the right direction. A step towards pushing down her fear of heights so that she could get on a plane again.

With a sigh, she sipped her drink, the bitter taste scalding her tongue. It was, in fact, an Irish coffee. "No," she replied finally, though of course, it wasn't the truth. Arden had only done as Rosie had asked. If she hadn't, Rosie would probably never have made it out of that forsaken tree.

"I only did as you asked." Arden elbowed Rosie in her ribs lightly, her eyes locked on the campfire flames. For whatever reason, Murray had decided he'd rather celebrate his birthday outside in the freezing night than in the nice warm cabin he and James must have paid a bomb for. Laughter and conversation hummed all around... it was a strange melody since Rosie hadn't been around so many people for so long. It reminded her of home, of New Year's Eve in the local pub. Rosie had spent this year's curled up on her tatty couch alone, listening to the fireworks and cheers outside her window, but at least she was here now. In the end, it hadn't been such a terrible first day of 2022 — minus the fact that she'd almost left behind half of her organs while coming down the zip line, that was.

"I know." Rosie blew out a breath and found the strength to smirk. Maybe it was the healthy dose of whiskey in her drink, but the orange glow guttering across Arden's face was mesmerising, and she couldn't find it in her to look away.

As though sensing her attention, Arden turned and her eyes locked onto Rosie's. They were murky and full of shadows in the darkness, but they sparkled with the same stars as the unpolluted air above.

"I think you did great, Rosie. I think you were really brave."

Rosie scoffed, her face burning with the last remnants of shame. She'd been a snotty, blubbering mess, and not just in front of Arden, but in front of her cocky ex-husband too. She bowed her head, cringing at the memory. She wished she could wipe it away with an eraser, like chalk on a blackboard. "I was awful. I'm really sorry for making such a scene. I probably embarrassed you just as much as I embarrassed myself."

"You didn't embarrass me. Why would you embarrass me?"

"Everyone thinks I'm your girlfriend." Rosie chewed on the inside of her cheek until she tasted blood. "That's embarrassing for you."

"Uh, thanks. But I'm not embarrassed." Arden shrugged, resting her elbows on her knees. Rosie almost shrank beneath the weight of her gaze. "In fact, I was pretty proud to be with you up there. Josh was being an asshole, and you were terrified, but you did it anyway. I wish I could face my fears that way."

Rosie's breath snagged in her throat at the words, spoken so softly, so sincerely. She didn't know what she'd done to deserve them, but it made her feel as though the hot, spiced Irish coffee she sipped had infiltrated her lungs, her chest, as well as her stomach. Like she was made of the stuff, a walking whiskey-laced, caffeine-buzzed, watery blob about to pour into the soil. She'd never felt that way before. She couldn't feel her knees or her toes, her ribs. She could only feel her pounding heart and that searing fire simmering through her. In it, she found the strength to ask, "What are you afraid of?"

Arden's focus flickered across the fire, suddenly saturated with a sadness that Rosie wanted nothing more than to chase away. She followed its direction instead — and found Quinn chugging down Jameson straight from the bottle. They'd got back from the zip line to find her tipsy on the couch with a few lawyer friends and Murray's step-son, Nathan, having helped themselves to Murray's well-stocked cupboard of liquor. Rosie had expected Arden to talk to her, but she'd said nothing, and it wasn't Rosie's business.

Now it seemed to be everyone's business. Quinn danced and laughed as animatedly as a cartoon character, but Rosie could see through it. She couldn't imagine what sort of pain Quinn must have been dealing with, and how that must have impacted Arden too. Why wasn't James doing more about it? Why had everyone just accepted Quinn's suffering, her drinking, her toxic relationship?

"Do you want to talk about it?" Rosie questioned gently.

Arden shrugged. "Our mom was an alcoholic. I couldn't blame her for it or anything. I know it's not her fault, but... it hurt us. It wasn't just the drinking either. She just seemed to stop caring about everything. She was a mess, and she couldn't take care of us, and even now, when she's in recovery, she just... isn't our mom anymore. And I'm worried that Quinn is on the same path." Her throat bobbed, and Rosie's own ached as though she felt the same pain. "I don't know how to get through to her. She dates awful people who treat her like shit, she drinks, and she acts like nothing she says or does has an effect on anyone else. Worse, Dad just sits by and lets her. I don't know what I'm supposed to do. I don't know how to stop it before it's too late."

"It's not your responsibility." Rosie couldn't help it. She placed down her mug and found Arden's hand. They were icy despite her grip on her own hot drink. "You can't fix her, Arden. Whatever it is or why Quinn acts the way she does... It's something she needs to work out alone. You can only try to help where you can."

Arden blinked, her glossy eyes sparkling with the promise of tears. "You're right. I'm just so sick of it. I'm sick of worrying. I'm sick of knowing that she's hurting and not knowing what to do about it. I..." She sucked in a shaky breath. "I should talk to her. Will you be okay here for a minute?"

Rosie nodded, nestling her chin further into her scarf. It was surprisingly toasty by the fire, and she found solace in watching the flames lick through the sky. "I'm here if you need me."

"Thank you." Arden rose, and Rosie waited to be left cold by her absence — but she wasn't. Not at first. Arden leaned in and placed a soft kiss on Rosie's temple, and it surprised Rosie enough that she turned to stone. Her heart froze in her chest. Her limbs forgot how to move. The fire seemed to hold its breath with her. Even the wind paused its journey through the rustling tree branches.

Realisation broke across Arden's features as she drew back, a hand rising to her bottom lip as though it had been as much of a surprise for her. Rosie could only stare, wide-eyed and shivery, and if she hadn't been liquid melting pathetically into the soil before, she sure as hell was now.

Arden blinked and then wandered off without another word, tugging on the hem of her fleecy jacket. Rosie could only sit, stunned, floating, grounded. The patch of skin that Arden's lips had touched still tingled as though the cells were brand new.

She'd kissed her like it had been in her nature to. Rosie might have written it off as part of their act, but nobody had been watching. It had just been the two of them, locked away in their own pocket of the woods.

Rosie wanted to stay there forever.

"Quinn. Can we talk?" Arden crunched her way through broken twigs and pine needles toward her sister, who still swayed with a bottle of

Jameson not too far from the riverbank.

Away from the fire, it was glacial, and goose pimples pricked beneath Arden's fleece sleeves against the bitter breeze. Their dad and Murray sat closer to the fire, chatting with Murray's co-workers — Josh included. But only Quinn, Aunt Gina, Nathan, and a couple of cousins braved the chairs furthest away, and it seemed they were all drinking with Quinn too. As though she needed enablers.

"About what?" Quinn asked. Her words were slurred and thick, and her breath reeked of sour liquor.

"In private, I mean." Arden dragged her away from their audience, further into the shadows of tall spruces.

"What's up?"

She raised an eyebrow. "I wanted to ask you the same question. You've been distant and I don't think I've seen you without a drink in your hand since I got here."

Quinn scoffed. "It's a birthday trip. Can't I have a little fun?"

"You're *always* having a little fun." Arden tried to keep the judgement from her tone, but it fringed her words all the same, leaving a rotten taste in her mouth.

"Oh, here we go." Quinn rolled her eyes and stumbled on unsteady feet. "One minute you couldn't give a shit less, and the next minute, you're all high and mighty and looking down your nose at me. Why don't you just mind your own business?"

Arden tensed, doing her best to school her features into a cool, neutral mask. It was another thing she'd grown tired of over the years, pretending that drunken words couldn't touch her and pretending that the way Quinn and her mom acted didn't leave her feeling blistered and raw and wrong.

"Because I'm worried about you," she uttered out through gritted teeth. "The way you act, the choices you make… they're so destructive."

Quinn scoffed, but with her puffed up cheeks and pursed lips, it seemed more as though she was blowing a raspberry. "I was sitting there minding my own business, Arden. *You're* the one who dragged me away from everyone to lecture me."

"I'm not *trying* to lecture you." Clamping down a curse, Arden pinched the bridge of her nose. "I'm just asking what's going on with you. It seems like you're getting bad again. Is it because of Leo? Because I saw the way he was with you at Christmas. He's no good for you, Quinn. You know that."

Another sneer, this time with twisted features that dripped with contempt. "We can't all find a fancy lawyer to marry or a sweet, ditzy little British woman to pretend to date. I'm sorry I'm not like you, Arden."

"No," Arden burst out before she could

stop herself. "No, you're like Mom. That's what's terrifying."

Quinn stilled, glaring at Arden through narrowed shadow-smudged eyes. "Is that what you think?"

Arden gestured to Quinn's frame as though it was obvious. "Is it not the truth?"

Upper lip curling into a snarl, Quinn muttered in a low, dangerous tone, "Fuck you, Arden."

She made to walk away, but Arden was desperate to make Quinn see, to understand her again, to help her. Her fingers curled around Quinn's cold wrist, and then she was thrust back by more force than she'd been prepared for. Whiskey swished out of Quinn's bottle and all over Arden's coat as she staggered back into marshy, slippery soil. She lost her footing. She was falling. Frantically, she grappled for Quinn's hand to keep her steady — but Quinn wasn't steady at all, and the two of them toppled from the banks together... into the icy, gushing river. Despite the cold, everything in Arden burned when the water submerged her: her skin, her bones, her blood. It stole the breath from her lungs, stole away her sight, until all that was left was a vacuum of black.

She didn't let it take her though. She kicked up her legs until she found the shallow, pebbled river bed. She rose to the surface, sputtering out foul-tasting, grainy water in disgust. Instinct left her searching for Quinn, and it didn't take long to glimpse her a few metres away, her peroxide-blonde hair matted to her face and her lips already stained blue.

"What the *fuck* is wrong with you?" Arden questioned through chattering teeth. The words scratched against a throat made of sandpaper.

She only realised too late that everybody was watching them now. Her dad stood at the forefront of it all, eyes wide in alarm. He rushed forward, crouching at the edge of the banks and offering out his hand. "You're going to catch your death in there. Both of you, out now!"

Arden didn't need telling twice. She forced her numb limbs to drive her forward, no longer caring if Quinn followed. Relief filled her when her dad's coarse hands curled around her own damp ones as he pulled her out. Her clothes dragged heavily on her weary shoulders and hips, leaving puddles in the soil as she marched away. She heard Quinn huffing her way back onto the banks too.

The embarrassment only came afterwards, when the eyes of a dozen different people, some strangers, some she wished was, scraping over her red-raw skin. She caught Murray's among them. "I'll talk to her," he murmured.

"She's beyond that." Arden's reply was fierce with rage. The only thing to quell it was Rosie standing behind her step-father, concern glistening in her eyes and lines wrinkling beneath her short bangs.

"Are you okay?"

Arden only shook her head, tears throbbing behind her eyes.

"Let's get you warm." With trembling fingers, Rosie unzipped her own coat and draped it across Arden's shoulders. She pinned it to her with her arm, guiding Arden into the cabin where her boots squelched onto the welcome mat.

When she caught her drenched, makeup-streaked reflection in the hallway mirror, she didn't recognise herself at all. And when she glimpsed Quinn making her way up the porch steps from the stairwell window, she didn't recognise her either.

The house was full of strangers — and then, among them, bundling Arden in towels and getting the shower running was Rosie.

Ten

@DesperatelySeekingStranger: HELP! I kissed the most perfect woman in the world on NYE, but I didn't get her number — or even her name. She's about 5'5 (with heels), brunette, a student at NYU majoring in art history, and she told me a story about her dog named Scampi peeing in her shoes before she left the house. We met in Black Flamingo and I think it was love at first sight, but how can I know if I can't find her? This is my last hope. If anybody knows her, please tell her that her New Year's kiss is looking for her!

The cabin was eerily silent when Rosie went back downstairs to make hot chocolate for Arden. Arden had gotten straight in the shower, and Rosie didn't know what else she could do to help — but a few sprinkles of marshmallows and cocoa powder would surely only make things better.

Exhausted and cold and still slightly confused about how Arden had ended up in the river, she gaped unseeingly at the steam curling from the pan of simmering milk. She missed kettles. Everything had been easier with kettles. Making a decent brew in America was a whole ordeal, and she didn't have the energy for it tonight.

The cabin at least stocked a few sachets of hot chocolate. She nabbed them from a small bowl and emptied them into two mugs before rooting for the marshmallows and cream. Luckily, Murray had brought both, though the marshmallows had been for toasting so they were slightly oversized.

"How's Arden doing?"

"Jesus!" The low voice breaking through the peaceful silence startled Rosie enough that she dropped the bag of marshmallows all over the floor. She pressed a hand to her chest, whipping around to find its owner. It was Josh, hovering at the corner of the breakfast bar.

"Sorry. I didn't mean to scare you. Here, let me help." He wandered over, kneeling to pick up the scattered marshmallows. Rosie let him. After the way he'd treated her earlier, it was the least he could do.

"She's okay, I think. She's warming up in the shower. Quinn?"

"Murray is handling her. She's always been a little unpredictable, but... I've never seen her like this." The marshmallows were flung into the bin under the sink — a waste, Rosie thought, as a perpetual advocate of the five-second rule. She salvaged the few that were left, pouring in the milk first and then topping it with whipped cream before dropping them in. The hot chocolate plopped as the marshmallows floated on top.

"Hot chocolate?" Rosie asked. There was just enough milk leftover, and Josh seemed concerned enough that her animosity towards him diminished.

"Sure. Why not?"

She retrieved a third mug from the cupboard and made him a drink too.

"Look, I owe you an apology," he said quietly.

It was enough to stop her mid-stir. She pulled the teaspoon from the mug slowly before looking at him. "I wasn't expecting one," she admitted.

"Well, you're getting one." Wryly, he scratched at a fair smattering of stubble across his cleft chin. "I'm not usually the jealous ex, I swear. I don't know what came over me today, but I was a complete ass and you didn't deserve it. The fact is…" he sighed as though preparing himself, "you make Arden happy, and that's not something I ever felt I could do. God knows I tried, but… I don't know. It never worked. Not the way it seems to with you."

The words were the last thing Rosie had been expecting, and she swallowed down her denial before it could surface, trying to forget for a moment that it was all an act. Maybe Josh didn't know Arden as well as he thought — or maybe he was telling the truth. Maybe Arden was happier now. If that was the case, Rosie doubted it had anything to do with her.

"Thank you," was all she said before

squirting the cream and adding the marshmallows to his drink. She extended the mug, a makeshift olive branch. He took it with an appreciative expression, sipping it so that he ended up with a cream moustache along his upper lip. Rosie choked on a laugh and then glanced upstairs. "I should get back."

"Right…" He waited until Rosie was leaving before he spoke again. "Rosie?"

Rosie turned back, the mug handles burning into her palms. "Hmm?"

"Is it serious between you two?"

She pondered the correct answer — the answer Arden would want Rosie to give — but she didn't know what it was. If they were still pretending, it was probably "no." But then, did non-serious couples act the way they had today? Did they feel the way Rosie felt when Arden looked at her? She didn't know. She'd never really done casual, and she'd never done pretend before now either.

Finally, she settled on the truth. "I hope so."

And then she padded back up to her bedroom still sparking with nerves. Arden was perched on the bed, wrapped in a colossal dressing gown with her hair wound into a towel. She was mid-yawn when Rosie entered, dangerously close to spilling the drinks.

"I thought you could do with a hot chocolate," she said, offering one of the mugs out. The cream had already melted and the marshmallows had dissolved into goo, but Arden took it all the same, curling her hands around the ceramic as though it was a lifeline.

"Thank you."

Rosie smiled and sat beside her, licking her lips. Droplets of water escaped from Arden's towel. They went down her cheeks, her jaw, and Rosie watched as though they were raindrops on a windowpane and she'd never seen the weather change before.

"How are you feeling? Better?"

"A little." Arden shrugged and bent one knee, leaving the other to dangle off the bed.

"Murray is with Quinn."

"Good. Somebody else should babysit her for a change." The bitterness surprised Rosie, but Arden's features flashed with instant regret. "Sorry. I'm just... exhausted."

"It's understandable. Family can be a pain in the arse."

"Yeah." Arden scoffed and took a slurp of her hot chocolate. She was careful not to make Josh's mistake and sink her face into the cream, but Rosie wasn't that graceful. Cream clung to her own lip, thick and sticky. She licked it off quickly.

"Josh just asked me if we were serious," she admitted. Though it was difficult, they were in this together — whatever *this* was. Besides, it was Arden's ex-husband. She had a right to know — even if it did make Rosie worry that maybe Arden would rekindle something with him.

With a surprised cough, Arden replied, "What did you tell him?"

"Well…" Dread rippled through Rosie, but still, she found the courage to meet Arden's eye, remembering the way Arden had kissed her on the temple earlier. It still seared her skin like a tattoo. "I told him that I hoped so."

"That's…" Arden's breath seemed to falter, just for a moment. Then she straightened, and her expression was neutral again. Rosie had no idea what any of it meant. "That's a good answer."

"I think he was asking because he still has feelings for you."

Arden only hummed, unravelling her hair from the towel. It cascaded down her back, a river of knotted, dark blonde waves. It wasn't at all fair that she looked so good after having just had a shower, with rosy, dewy skin.

For some reason, Rosie couldn't let the topic float away with Arden's dismissal. "I think maybe he was hoping I'd said no," she continued, "so he could swoop in."

"Well, then thank God you said yes."

"It's not really any of my beeswax but… what happened between you two? Why did you get a divorce?"

Arden sighed, wringing her hair out a final time before leaving it be. "We just didn't work. It didn't feel right. I think maybe I married him because I thought it was the right thing to do. I think… I think I wanted that sort of stability, and I romanticised it all in my head so much — the nice house and the fancy dinner parties and all that — that I just ended up disappointed when I realised I didn't *only* care about those things. Because in the end, they were all I got from him, and it wasn't enough. We didn't have a connection. He didn't care about my work, and I didn't care about his, and we ran out of things to talk about ten minutes after I walked down the aisle. We were always too busy for each other, and when we weren't, I found myself wishing I was somewhere else. Josh is a decent guy most of the time, but... that's all I found in him, y'know? Just a decent guy. Then I realised I didn't need anyone else to feel stable anyway. My business took off, and I was happy in the studio all day, and all the marriage really was for me was making up for something I should have had as a kid. Something I can give myself. So that's what I did."

Knowing the truth set Rosie at ease. Arden spoke about Josh blankly, as though she held no feelings for him whatsoever. It meant Rosie didn't have to worry. It meant... Well, she didn't know what it meant, but hope soared through her belly all the same.

"Anyway. I'm exhausted." Arden yawned again. "I need my pyjamas."

Pyjamas sounded heavenly. Rosie got up to find her own and cringed when she only found a bunch of jumpers, leggings, and phone chargers in her bag. "Oh, bugger. I think I had a complete brain fart while I was packing. I can't find my PJs."

She tugged out a sweatshirt instead, glad that it was one that drowned her. She only had to worry about bottoms now. Leggings would do.

"You're not going to wear those to bed, are you?" Arden asked, eyeing the tight, black jersey material gripped in her hands.

"I don't have anything else." Rosie worried at her lip.

"Are they comfy?"

Rosie considered them. For daytime, they were fine, but she didn't particularly like suffocating her legs all night. She shrugged. "They'll do."

Arden's expression remained unconvinced, but Rosie scampered into the en suite bathroom and got dressed, glad that she'd at least brought her toothpaste and a hairbrush. She scraped her makeup away, though most of it had rolled off with her tears earlier, and then emerged in her non-pyjamas. They weren't comfy at all, actually. She'd brought the leggings where the waistband dug into her stomach, and she was already bloated and aching from the anxiety of the day, not to mention the number of hot drinks she'd consumed.

Arden was already tucked into bed. Rosie hovered uncertainly at the foot, eyeing the armchair by the window and wondering if she was expected to sleep there.

"What are you doing?"

"I just... I don't know where to sleep."

"Well," Arden's arm appeared above the duvet to pat down the other side of the bed, "See this big thing here? This is usually where people sleep."

"You don't mind sharing?"

"As long as you don't hog the covers." Arden sank down again, though her eyes remained open as Rosie carefully slipped into the other side.

It was the warmest place she'd been all day, and she basked in it. The smell of fresh linen curled around her along with Arden's floral shampoo. It was all so cosy and clean and homely. Maybe it wasn't just the warmest place Rosie had been all day. Maybe it was the warmest place she'd been all her life. It certainly felt that way as she relaxed into the mattress, pillowing her head with her hand as she turned on her side to face Arden. Arden was still looking at her, watching, as though Rosie was a movie she couldn't press pause on.

"I'm glad you were here today," she finally admitted.

"I'm glad I was here too," Rosie admitted. "Sort of, anyway. Minus the zip line trauma."

It was a lie. Rosie couldn't think of one place in the world she'd rather be than here, now, under the duvet with a woman who had once been a stranger but now felt like something so much more.

A choked chortle fell from Arden, and her eyes crinkled at the corners. Rosie would have joined in, but her waistband only felt tighter now that she was laying down. "I lied before. The leggings aren't comfy."

"Then take them off." Arden's whisper left heat knotting itself through Rosie's stomach. She didn't have it in her to argue.

"I'm wearing underwear," Rosie reassured. "Promise."

And the sweater hit her thighs, anyway. It wouldn't be all that promiscuous, would it? She didn't care if it was. She peeled the leggings off under the duvet and flung them onto the floor, breathing a sigh of relief.

"As long as they're not the same ones you peed in earlier."

Rosie had most likely let a small drop of wee slip out on the zip line and had said as much when Arden had met her on the other side. She wrinkled her nose at the memory now. Still, Arden's leg found hers and hooked itself around her calf, her smooth foot brushing against Rosie's prickles. Winter meant no leg shaving, but perhaps she should have bent the rules a little bit. She just hadn't expected... this.

If Arden minded, she didn't show it. Instead, her eyes fluttered shut.

"I didn't *actually* wee in my knickers." Rosie thought it vital to reassure before Arden drifted off. "Just making that known."

Arden smirked sleepily but her lids remained sealed. "Hmm," she hummed.

"Whatever you say."

Eleven

Arden was running late. It had been a disaster of a
day, starting with oversleeping, which had left all
of her classes half an hour behind schedule, and
ending with trying to pick up her phone, which
she had clumsily dropped in the toilet last night,
from the repair shop. She'd found out there that it
was beyond help, so she would have to get a new
one.

Still, there was no way in hell that she
would miss Rosie's mixer, and she'd whipped
around her bedroom like a cyclone, throwing on
a shimmery dress that she had planned to wear

for New Year's Eve before Murray had invited her to his birthday weekend instead. Her makeup was rushed, eyeliner wonky, and there was no time to do anything with her hair save for throwing it up into a neat bun and attacking it with so much hairspray that she ended up dizzy and coughing. After a light spritz of perfume and a swipe of lip gloss, she glimpsed herself in the mirror and cringed at her flustered reflection.

It was too late to fix now.

As Arden gathered a pale blue clutch that definitely did not match her dress, a knock rattled through her apartment. Her heart stuttered with the hope, the expectation, that Rosie stood on the other side of the door.

But it wasn't Rosie hovering in the poorly-lit hallway.

It was Quinn — and she looked awful. Mascara had smeared down her face in streaks, her bleached hair was a tangle of knots, and her complexion was a ghastly white save for a few splotches of red. It was a telltale sign that she'd been crying. A lot.

Stunned, Arden could only stumble back. She hadn't talked to Quinn since Murray's birthday getaway, still seething — and, worse, heartbroken — over the way Quinn had acted in the face of Arden's concern. Murray and their dad had finally taken to paying attention, and Quinn had been spending a lot of time out in Westhampton. Now she was here, but it wasn't really her. It was a sobbing wreck of a stranger, and Arden didn't know what to do.

"Quinn…"

"I'm sorry." Tears leaked from Quinn's eyes as her chest heaved. "I'm so sorry, Arden. You were right. You were right about everything. I'm awful. I'm a mess. I'm sorry."

Dread wrenched through Arden's stomach. She pulled Quinn into her arms, any bitterness evaporating to make way for bone-splintering worry. "What happened? What's wrong?"

"He's sleeping with Savannah. My best fucking friend. He's awful, and I always knew it. I don't know why I stayed. I don't know why I always stay." Quinn's grip was bruising, like a child clinging onto their comfort blanket for dear life, afraid of the monsters under their bed. Arden winced, kicking the door shut with her foot. She had nosy neighbours on the best of days. They didn't need to witness this.

"I don't know either," Arden admitted. She didn't know how it had come to this. She didn't know anything. She could only pull Quinn down to the couch and hand her a paint-stained paper towel to wipe her eyes with, left out from patterning her latest vase.

Snotty and soggy, Quinn blew her nose, still shuddering, still unrecognisable. But still Arden's sister, somewhere in there. Arden should have tried harder. She should have talked to Quinn sooner. She'd despised Leo from the moment she'd met him… but Quinn was stubborn and unreachable, just like their mom. She didn't want to see the truth. Arden had played the disapproving, lecturing sister more than enough times to know that it only ever drove them apart. But she should have done *something*.

"There's something wrong with me," Quinn continued. "But… But I don't want to be like this anymore, Arden. I don't want you to hate me anymore. I'm so fucking sick of myself."

"I don't hate you, Quinn." Arden's own eyes pricked with tears now. She squeezed Quinn's frail arm, sniffling. "I just miss my sister, that's all. I just want you to be safe and healthy and happy."

Quinn's smile was wobbly, wrong. "So do I."

"So tell me how to help." It was a plea, raw and hoarse in Arden's throat.

"I don't know." Quinn wiped her eyes with trembling fingers, choking on an embarrassed laugh. "What if you can't help me? What if I'm always going to be like her?"

"The fact you're here, telling me that's not what you want, is already a step in the right direction. You're not like her, Quinn." Arden cupped Quinn's jaw in her palm, catching the tears as they fell. And she saw then that it was true: Quinn wasn't their mom. She'd inherited her problems because she'd been exposed to them, just like Arden had become fiercely independent and barely ever let loose at all. They were the complete opposite of one another. They were two sides of the same coin, she and her sister. Two different outcomes of the same equation. Quinn didn't want to be this way, but growing up, it was all she'd known. As the older child, she'd seen more of it too. The worst of it. It had driven away their brother as soon as he'd had the chance to get out, but Quinn and Arden had handled it differently.

Arden had to stop blaming Quinn. She had to stop resenting her for her suffering just because it presented itself differently from Arden's. She had to help Quinn however she could if she wanted to keep her sister, her family. She loved her too much to lose her.

Quinn's eyes fluttered closed, her chin trembling. "Can I live here for a while? I know I could go to Dad's, but…"

But their dad understood it even less than Arden did. He'd had his share of heartache from their mom, and he always stood five steps away from it now, pretending that he couldn't see it because it was too hard to bear otherwise. It wasn't right. He should have been better. They all should have. But it was just how he coped, and Arden couldn't blame him for it.

She sucked in a deep breath and nodded. "Yes. You can stay for as long as you want. But no more of this, Quinn. No more drinking. No more shitty friends and boyfriends. You need to take care of yourself, and I can't keep watching you do the opposite."

Quinn nodded. "I will. I *want* to be better. I

mean it. No more drinking. No more Leo. I'll find a job to pay my share of the rent, and I'll spend every night on the couch watching those fancy British period dramas you like with you. I'll do my best, Arden. I'll be a better sister and a better person. I just... I need help."

Maybe she was naive and maybe it would end up hurting her in the end, but Arden found herself believing Quinn. She clasped Quinn's clammy hands and said, "Then I'll help you. We'll figure it all out together."

Relief caused Quinn to slump. She rested her head against Arden's chest, just like when they were kids — only then, it had been Arden seeking comfort in her big sister when she'd had a nightmare or when their mom had come home drunk again and started trashing the house.

She'd forgotten those moments, painted pink by their owl night light, listening to the sound of her sister's heartbeat to muffle out the shouts downstairs. Quinn had been a sturdy rock against a crashing tempest. Now, she needed Arden to be the same for her.

The sequins of Arden's dress rustled as Quinn shifted and then drew away, her eyes roaming Arden's clothes. "You were going somewhere. God, I'm sorry. Where were you going?"

"It's just a mixer for that app," Arden brushed off, though a pang of guilt shot through her as she imagined Rosie there without her. She would understand, Arden knew. If she was who Arden thought she was, she'd understand. "Rosie invited me, but it's okay. I'm sure she'll manage without me."

"No." Quinn closed her eyes, and when she opened them, they blazed with determination. "No, you deserve to be happy. You should go. I'll be okay here."

There was no way Arden was going anywhere, and she showed as much by narrowing her eyes. "It's fine. I'll catch up with her another day. I think there's ice cream in the freezer. Go get it, and I'll put on my PJs then we can watch a movie."

"No, Arden." Quinn's features grew taut, pleading. "You know, I've never seen you smile and laugh as much as you do with her. She makes you happy. I just… I don't want to ruin it. Go have fun with her."

"You don't ruin it. Besides, it's just a stupid fake date —"

Quinn rolled her eyes, cutting Arden off. "Yeah, right. She looks at you like you're… I don't know… one of those delicious fruity cocktails that always come with an umbrella *and* a sparkler. *Please*, Arden. I'll be okay here. It'll give me a chance to clear my head. You were right earlier. I've been self-sabotaging, but I've also been fucking up with everyone else too. Especially you. You said you wanted me to be happy. I only want the same for you. So let's be happy for each other, okay?

Also, more than anything, I want to catch up on *Grey's Anatomy* and you just complain whenever you watch it with me."

Arden scoffed. "Don't think you'll be taking over my TV now that you live here."

Quinn's features remained intense, scolding. "Go and get your girl. And then bring me back pizza as a gift for setting you up in the first place."

"Will you be here when I get back?" Arden was unable to keep the doubt from seeping in. She didn't know if she could trust Quinn anymore. What if Arden left her alone and she just ended up going back to Leo or the nearest bar?

"I'm not a kid, Ard, and I meant what I said. I'm going to be okay... eventually. I'm at least going to try. You can take the apartment key if it makes you feel better."

Arden rolled her eyes. She wanted her sister safe, but not if it meant becoming a prison warden. If she wanted to trust Quinn, she had to start somewhere. She had to give her a chance. So Arden sighed and stood up to smooth the creases from her dress. "Are you sure?"

"Positive. Go away. Also, I'm still going to eat your ice cream."

If it kept Quinn away from the shadows, Arden would keep her freezer stocked for the rest of time. "Okay."

"Okay." Quinn smiled, shaky and weak, and Arden almost sat back down. Quinn had other ideas, though. She rose to shoo Quinn away, ushering her towards the door and shoving her purse back into her hands. "Go on. My McDreamy awaits me, as does yours. Oh, and maybe tell Rosie how you really feel. *Cheerio*. Goodbye. Bye."

"I'm not taking relationship advice from you," Arden grumbled as she fell out of the apartment.

"*Byeeeeeee*." Quinn closed the door, and Arden heard the bolt clicking into place. She thought of the key in her purse. She could still lock it, still keep Quinn from ever getting hurt again, but...

No. She couldn't. She couldn't protect her sister from the bad things. She could only support her now and hope that Quinn was being genuine in her desire to get better. There was only one way to find that out though, but Arden couldn't waste any more time pondering over it.

Rosie was waiting for her. It was time to go.

Twelve

@MaytheForce: Getting ready for the mixer! So excited to meet my favourite person in the world @PrincessLeah and finally see her beautiful face. The stars are watching us tonight, Lee. I can feel it.

Rosie felt as though she was plunging off the zip wire all over again as she stepped into the function room that Caroline had hired for the Don't Be a Stranger's mixer event. Strobe lights painted the dance floor with splotches of lilac and pink, and a DJ had set himself up onstage though the music hadn't started yet. After pinning a name badge in the shape of an envelope sealed by a heart to her dress and labelling herself "Rosie, AKA LookingforLove" in red Sharpie, she checked her phone for the billionth time that day and sighed. Arden hadn't texted her since yesterday, and Rosie had no idea if she was still coming. She'd even considered poking her head into the pottery studio that morning on her way to work but thought that might have looked too desperate.

Clearly, Arden was ignoring her. Maybe she'd lost interest. Maybe their deal was over. Rosie hadn't let herself confront those possibilities yet because she knew that the small whisper of desolation in her gut would turn into an almighty roar if she did. Besides, she didn't have time to be sad tonight.

A wolf whistle tore her attention from the tacky decorations. She found Wade by the bar, two fingers in his grinning mouth. In the dappled lighting, his teeth were an aggressively fluorescent white. "You look *hot*, Rosie Gladwell!"

She looked down at her dress and tugged the frilly hem hesitantly. She didn't know if she looked hot enough to deserve Wade's compliment-slash-harassment, but she had put in effort tonight — both to look her best for her boss and also on the off-chance Arden did remember the invitation.

"Thank you." Rosie scuttled over to the group of co-workers, glad when Wade handed her a pink cocktail. A Cosmo, she found upon her first sip.

"When's your date arriving?"

Rosie shrugged. "I don't know if she is. I haven't heard from her today. I think maybe something has come up. Or maybe she changed her mind. I don't know."

Wade's brows furrowed with concern, and he pinched Rosie's elbow to tug her away from the others. "What do you mean she changed her mind? Why would she change her mind? When did you last see her?"

Rosie counted the days. Arden had met up with her for lunch last Friday, and they'd gone for a coffee between Arden's pottery classes on Sunday but... it had been mostly radio silence since. Rosie had spent the week racking her brain as to why. Had she said or done something stupid? Probably. But she was also worried. Maybe Arden was dealing with problems with Quinn, and Rosie was just selfish for assuming it was about her. Still, she couldn't help but voice her concern.

"Sunday. Maybe she's gotten bored of me or something. Maybe she doesn't want me anymore." As a pretend girlfriend or anything else. After all, Rosie had fulfilled her end of the bargain. She'd shown her face twice for the sake of Arden's family. Maybe Arden just... didn't need her anymore.

"*Pfft*. Nobody could ever be bored of you. I'm certain she'll show up." He pointed to the door. "Speaking of, here they come."

Rosie turned on her dangerously tall heels. A crowd spilt into the room, some of them in groups and others alone. The DJ welcomed them in over a remix of "I Want to Know What Love Is" by Foreigner, which Rosie found terribly cheesy. It was strange to see so many faces. Rosie wondered which of them used the app regularly. Had she scrolled past their posts, commented on them, even, before?

"Enough jabbering amongst yourselves." The stern voice came from behind, cutting through the buzzing excitement floating in from the new guests. Rosie found it belonged to Caroline and something inside her lurched with the need to recoil. What would she tell her if Arden didn't show up tonight? "Let's go and welcome our guests, shall we?"

Rosie nodded meekly, smoothing down her dress a final time in the hopes it might also smooth down her nerves. Maybe she could just pick someone from the crowd and ask them to go along with it. It was practically the way their relationship — *non*-relationship, she reminded herself — had started.

If she wanted to save her job tonight, she'd have to figure something out. So she did as Caroline asked. She socialised. And as she did, her spirit wilted more and more. She met the couple she'd witnessed the first meeting of in Washington Square Park, *and* she bumped into PretzelLover89, who, thank the stars, was not in costume tonight and had brought a date he'd met on the app. She introduced herself to people who, understandably, wished to keep their identity anonymous. Those who didn't mind revealing their identity had marked their username on their pin badges like Rosie, and some of them were familiar.

But none of them was Arden, and Rosie's hope dwindled with her energy as the hour passed.

"Rosie!" She was grabbed from an awfully dull conversation about Minecraft with

GamerGuy00 and was met with Caroline's harsh features. She placed her hands on her hips expectantly. "Your speech is in five minutes. Are you ready?"

No. Rosie's heart racketed against her ribs painfully as she glanced at the stage. *Oh, God.* This would be a new level of embarrassment. She was about to preach about true love as a woman who had offered herself up as a pretend date, only to get stood up by her. "I have my speech, but —"

Caroline wasn't listening. Her eyes were darting around. "Where's your date? Go and fetch them before we get started."

"Well, that's what I'm trying to tell you." Rosie scratched her arm awkwardly, sinking beneath her sadness. Arden hadn't come. She wasn't here. A part of her had held out hope, but... it was all over now. "My date isn't —"

"Here!" Breathless and stumbling, Arden appeared beside Caroline, clutching her side in pain. "I'm here!"

"*Arden*?" Rosie frowned in surprise, elation singing through her blood. She was here. She was really here — and despite her state, she looked beautiful, in a sparkling cocktail dress and light, shimmery makeup.

"I'm so sorry. I dropped my phone in the toilet last night, and then I meant to catch you on your way to work but I overslept this morning, and then Quinn turned up at my apartment — "

"This is *TequilaGirl*?" Caroline questioned,

her gaze dragging along Arden from head to toe. "Well, what else can I expect with a username like that? As long as the two of you can look happy and in love for the rest of the night, I don't care. Now get up on stage, Rosie. We're ready for you. And TequilaGirl, go and get a name badge."

Rosie opened her mouth to protest, but Caroline was already sauntering away towards the bar. Rosie should have spent more time there too. Now she was very sober and was about to stand up in front of a room full of people. She turned to Arden, her lips parting with worry.

"I'm really sorry," Arden repeated, scraping her hair back nervously. "I'm awful. You should yell at me."

"I don't have time to yell at you." Rosie only had time to hyperventilate as the music faded out and Ning introduced herself as the Executive Director of Don't Be a Stranger. "I'm just really glad you're here to witness the train wreck I'm about to become."

"You're not going to be a train wreck." Arden placed her hands on Rosie's shoulders, and Rosie let out a breath as though her lungs had been waiting to see Arden again, to feel her. She didn't have time to think about what that meant either. "You're going to be wonderful. You don't even have to lie. Just tell them you met an amazing, fabulous, wonderful person online, and now here you are. Here *we* are."

Rosie snorted, clutching Arden's hands.

"...And next, we want to share with you our very own success story from our marketing specialist, who managed to find true love on Don't Be a Stranger, just as we hope the rest of you will. Rosie Gladwell, everybody."

The room erupted with applause, but Rosie barely heard it because of the roaring in her ears. She felt Arden push her forward, and then she was stepping onto the stage beneath a hazy lavender spotlight. A sea of unfamiliar faces stared back at her. She had never imagined that when she posted on Don't Be a Stranger, this was the reality of it. A bunch of strangers, all listening, all relying on her.

She took a breath and tried to remember the speech she'd been rehearsing all day.

∞∞∞

Arden held her breath as Rosie glided — well, stumbled, really — into the bright spotlight in the centre of the stage. Her hands were cold and clammy though she didn't know why. *She* wasn't the one who had to speak in front of hundreds of people, thank heavens.

Static sliced through the din of low murmurs as Rosie grabbed the microphone from its stand, wincing. "Oh, shit, sorry!"

A few chuckles rang out at the expletive. Arden glanced at Rosie's boss and found her looking less than impressed by the bar with her arms crossed over her chest and her lips pursed.

"Come on, Rosie," Arden whispered under her breath. "You can do it."

"Sorry, pardon my French!" Rosie apologised quickly, her voice beginning crackly but ending clear. She pasted a false smile onto her face before offering a coy wave. "Hi, everyone. I'm Rosie, AKA *LookingforLove*. I'm a marketing specialist for Don't Be a Stranger, but that's not why I'm here to talk to you today."

She gulped a deep breath, and Arden couldn't help but do the same.

"I'm sure a lot of you know that New York can be a lonely place," Rosie continued. "It's big and intimidating — a bit like the guy she tells you not to worry about. Am I right, folks?" The joke earned a few — and only a few — laughs. "Okay, tough crowd. Anyway, like most of you, I signed up to Don't Be a Stranger to find... something. I didn't really know what at the time. I just knew that I wasn't finding it at work or on the subway or in coffee shops like they usually do in the movies. I wanted to *talk* to people. I wanted to *meet* people. I tried my hand at dating, both on and off the app, but nothing ever really worked out." Rosie tucked her hair behind her ears as her gaze fell to Arden. She squinted, shielding her eyes from the colourful lights with a shaky hand. "Until I commented on a post by *TequilaQueen*, who was searching for a date for Christmas."

A stream of *awws* rang out, and Arden's

cheeks burned when a few people turned to look at her. She nodded, greeting them awkwardly before focusing on Rosie again — and the picture projected on the screen behind her. It was a collage of posts and comments from Don't Be a Stranger: Quinn's first advertisement, made while tipsy at a bottomless brunch, and Rosie's replies expressing her interest.

There was another post though. One Arden had never seen before, dated 12th December.

@LookingforLove: *Dear potter on E 12th Street,*

I pass your studio each day on my commute to work and always, without fail, am reminded of that one scene in Ghost. *You know the one — with the wheel and the clay and Patrick Swayze's wonderful hands. That is to say, I think both you and your work are quite lovely and well worth the extra five minutes it takes for me to pass through your block before getting to the subway. I just thought you should know.*

Love,
Anon

Arden's insides felt as though she was plunging down an unpredictable, fifty-foot rollercoaster. *LookingforLove* was Rosie, and Arden's pottery studio was on East 12th — but Rosie couldn't have known that days before they'd met for the first time.

But that meant that Rosie had been

attracted to Arden before all of this. It meant... It meant that Rosie had already known Arden. Why hadn't she said something?

Arden's knees wobbled as everything pieced together. She used to hate these sorts of posts: secret admirers, people posting about random strangers just because they found them attractive. But there was nothing creepy or unsettling about Rosie's words. She'd only said that Arden and her work were quite lovely. She'd only made it clear that Rosie had *noticed* Arden.

And Arden wanted Rosie to notice her.

It was... romantic. Completely, utterly, tooth-rottingly sweet. It left Arden reeling with the room spinning and the lights brightening. She felt a swirl of sunlight and warmth burning through her gut, through her chest. She forgot to listen to what Rosie was saying. She forgot everything, only able to wonder how many times Rosie had walked past her studio and glimpsed Arden through the window. How many times had Arden seen a short-haired, vibrantly-dressed woman pass her, not knowing that the stranger was about to change something vital in her life? That she would become something so much more than just another faceless person in a crowded city?

Arden had never believed in chance or fate or the universe, but the serendipity she marvelled at now swallowed her whole, until she was floating with the Don't Be a Stranger-branded helium balloons that were grazing the ceiling.

"Anyway, what I suppose I'm trying to say is..." Rosie was still talking, and Arden had forgotten to listen. "Don't Be a Stranger isn't just a dating app. Not for me, anyway. It isn't based on the superficial. You're allowed to be anyone you want to be there, *talk* to anyone you want, and it was that that gave me the courage to meet *TequilaQueen*. I found something special the day I agreed to meet her, and I've seen other people find it too."

The slides projected behind her flicked to other people's posts: tales of first meetings, dates being set, lives being lived, and connections being found.

"It's designed for blind dating, but it's also more than that. It's a social media app, one that celebrates diversity and happiness and friendship as well as romantic love. It made me realise that there are so many wonderful people to meet — and I was lucky enough to find one who I really connected with." Rosie found Arden in the crowd again, the corner of her mouth twitching with a smile. "It wasn't expected, and it wasn't planned, but it gave me hope again. It made me feel brave. *LookingforLove* doesn't have to look anymore, and I know that the rest of you will be just as lucky, too, if you give it a chance. Thank you."

The audience erupted in applause, some of them even swiping tears from their eyes. Arden wasn't too far from doing the same. She clasped her clammy hands together, and her heart leaped into her throat as Rosie stepped off the stage. Arden's lips parted, but her words had been stolen, her mind unable to form a sentence above the echoes of emotion reverberating through her.

"Congratulations, Rosie." It was Rosie's boss, looking pleased as she placed a thin hand on Rosie's shoulder. "I think you've earned yourself a promotion. Let's talk about next steps on Monday, shall we? Don't Be a Stranger needs a face for the brand, and you might just be perfect."

Rosie's eyes widened. She nodded, her mouth agape as Caroline smiled and wandered away. As soon as she was out of earshot, Rosie turned to Arden. "What just happened?"

Arden's cheeks almost tore from the force of her grin. "I think you just got a well-deserved promotion from your boss."

"I didn't do anything," Rosie murmured, dazed. "I just... I didn't do anything."

"I think you did plenty." Arden shook her head, softening as she inched closer. "Why didn't you tell me that you already knew who I was?"

Snapping back to attention, Rosie's brows furrowed. "What?"

Of course. She hadn't seen the screen. She probably had no idea the post had been there, behind her.

"They showed one of your older posts. You were admiring a potter on East 12th Street."

The shock trickled across Rosie's features in

gradual stages, starting with the crinkling of her forehead and ending with her mouth covered by her hands. She cringed away from Arden. "Oh, God. No. *Nonono*. This is awful. You must think I'm a creep. I am a creep, aren't I? I didn't know it was you until you told me about your studio, I swear! I'm not a stalker. I'm not."

With a light chuckle, Arden prised Rosie's hands away from her face. "I don't think you're a stalker. I think it's sweet. I think *you're* sweet. *Quite lovely*, actually."

Rosie's face flushed to match the red and purple strobe lights. "*Stop*," she groaned.

"I mean it." Arden had to shout to be heard over the music as the room bustled to life again. She didn't want to shout. Not to say what she wanted to. She wanted to show Rosie the same goodness, the same silk-softness, that Rosie had shown her. So she pulled her out of the room by the hand, into an echoey, dimly lit hallway, where the party was only a muffled memory.

A draught whispered around the room here, and Arden covered her arms with her hands tightly, fighting down a shiver. Rosie still wouldn't look at her.

"Rosie," Arden whispered desperately. "Don't be embarrassed."

"I *am* embarrassed. We were just supposed to pretend, but I... I liked you before I even knew you. I wasn't pretending at all. I mean, look at you. You're like a magical potter fairy, and I'm just the weirdo looking into your window. Oh, my God. I'm a peeping Tom."

"Why do you see yourself like that?" Arden's brows knitted together again. "That's not how it was."

Rosie bowed her head, tugging at a loose thread on the belt loop of her dress. "But it's how it must seem to you."

"No. You said you didn't know it was me when we first met. I trust you."

"I didn't. I only ever saw your outline through the window — maybe your hair and the vases on display. But never your face. I only put it all together in the bakery, when you told me you owned the studio, and then I thought it would be better not to tell you that I already had some sort of catastrophic crush on you. I'm sorry, Arden. This is weird."

"It's *not* weird," Arden denied, stepping closer and lacing her fingers through Rosie's. "It's not weird because... I wasn't pretending with you either. I liked you from the minute I met you. It was like I just knew... you were right. I didn't even have to try. We just fell into place, where we were supposed to be."

Surprise danced in Rosie's eyes as they snagged on Arden. "What are you saying?"

"I'm saying that you're brave and kind and warm and hilarious, and I want to be with you. For real. I don't want to pretend that we're pretending anymore. I just want to be what we've been from the beginning, and I want it to stay that way for a long, long time. I'm saying," hungrily, Arden glanced at Rosie's plump lips, painted a velvety red tonight, "that I want to kiss you now."

An elated giggle bubbled from Rosie, and then her lips belonged to Arden, and Arden's belonged to Rosie. They swayed against each other as they sealed whatever magic had formed between them in such a short space of time. Arden kissed like it was not just the first time, but the last time too, and while it made her feel new and different and paramount, it also felt like the most normal, most natural thing in the universe.

They weren't strangers anymore and now, Arden had time to make sure they never would be again. Rosie was the only person Arden wanted, and finally, she had found her.

Maybe she'd been looking for love too all this time, just in the wrong places. Not anymore. She was home now. For the first time in her life, she was home. No pretending. No doubts. Nothing but Rosie, holding her hand; Rosie kissing her; Rosie threading her fingers through Arden's hair.

"Will your boss take back the promotion if we leave early?" Arden finally asked breathlessly as she fiddled with a button on Rosie's dress.

Rosie shook her head, pink-cheeked and swollen-lipped. "No."

"Good. Let's go."

Thirteen

@BlushinginBrooklyn: All is not lost. The yoga instructor I'm in love with (see previous post) turned up to the mixer tonight and bought me a drink. Discovered that it is easier to flirt with her when I am not in Downward Dog. Think I have a chance now. Wish me luck. Namaste.

It was the first time that Rosie had actually been inside Arden's pottery studio. The pastel colours of the painted clay were brighter in here than they'd ever looked through the window — and so was Arden. She was a shimmer in the middle of the shadows as she turned on the lamp on the corner of her workbench, leaving the room crisscrossed with silver moonlight and rich amber.

Rosie knew it was an image she'd always remember: a memory she would stamp forever on her brain. A few weeks ago, she'd been on the outside looking in — love was but a distant fantasy, all of her dates terribly unsuccessful, and hope slowly dwindling. Now she was here, with the one person who had caught her eye from the moment she'd first walked past her. It was surreal.

Wonderful. Rosie was afraid that she was in a dream, and if she moved too quickly, spoke too loudly, it would all shatter and she'd surface back to the real world of grey days and lonely nights.

But then Arden hunched over the computer at the front desk, her features smooth and glowing in the light of the screen, and a moment later, music drifted through the studio.

Rosie laughed, loudly, but the dream didn't break. "'Unchained Melody'."

"Is this Patrick Swayze enough for you?" Arden smirked, rounding the front desk again and pulling a stool up to her pottery wheel.

Rosie stopped her, curling her hands around Arden's wrists and pulling her away. She didn't want to make pottery tonight. There'd be time for that. So much time. Instead, she drew Arden into a kiss. Rosie's fingers danced at the nape of Arden's bare neck. Arden gripped Rosie's waist, pressing their bodies together, leaving Rosie feverish with want.

"I don't want Patrick Swayze anymore," Rosie whispered, resting her forehead against Arden's. "I just want you."

"I'm already yours. I was before I even knew it."

Yours. Nobody had ever been Rosie's to claim before now. She'd allowed herself to belong to other people, and then she'd spent a long time as no one's at all, but nobody had ever made her feel as though she was important, as though she was an equal.

Nobody but Arden. It still surprised Rosie how willing Arden was to give herself completely — but it made sense. She'd welcomed Rosie into her home, her life, her heart, and Rosie had tried her best to do the same tonight. The speech hadn't been a lie. None of it had ever been a lie, no matter how this had started.

Something had brought them together: fate, or geography, or Don't Be a Stranger, or Quinn, or just plain coincidence, Rosie didn't know, but she was grateful, and she wouldn't take advantage of her newfound good luck.

She'd keep Arden close because everything felt better that way. That's what she did now, in the pottery studio. She tugged Arden close and looped her arms around her neck, and they swayed along to a song from a movie like they were the main characters, and Rosie fell and fell and fell, just as she had been from the beginning.

She wasn't afraid to anymore because Arden was hers. Rosie would climb any height and face any fear to keep it that way.

Epilogue

@RosieFoundLove: About to face my fears head-on. If I can fall in love with a stranger, I can do anything... right?

Love,
Rosie

"I can't do it, Arden." Rosie clutched onto the bannister for dear life, a cold sweat glistening above her brows. She'd just about managed the elevator, but now her knees were beginning to tremble with the knowledge that in a moment, she'd be out in the open, three hundred and twenty metres from the ground.

A little bit higher than the tree she'd climbed and cried at the top of just a few weeks ago.

"I think you can," Arden replied, patiently crossing her arms over her chest. "I think you can do anything."

"I think you overestimate me."

"I think you *under*estimate yourself." She gave Rosie a stern look and then offered out a hand. "I'll be with you the entire time. Do you think I'd let you fall?"

"No." Rosie swallowed, a thick lump of fear lodged in her throat — not for falling, she'd come to realise, but for the unsteadiness that heights brought. It was easier on the ground. She didn't have to think about what was beneath her. But there was something awfully surreal about being closer to the sky, the clouds, so far away from the world she knew.

In short, she thought too much.

She shuffled closer to the railings as a couple passed her on the steps, casting her curious looks as they climbed. She returned them with a tentative grin and then continued pouting when they disappeared.

"Then what are you afraid of?" Arden asked.

Rosie sucked in a breath and admitted, "I don't know. I just freak out."

"Because you're stuck in a cycle. You're letting it hold you back. Everybody clings onto some form of fear because if we didn't, everything would feel too easy, too good to be true. But if you took a breath and saw all the things you've missed, I think you'd be surprised."

"I'm being therapised against my will." She huffed dramatically, though she knew Arden was only trying to help. But stopping to enjoy the view was easier said than done, especially when the view in question made Rosie dizzy and breathless and close to throwing up. She didn't even know why she was here. It had seemed like a good idea an hour ago, when she'd just gotten off the phone with her mum and had realised that she missed her family so much it made her ache. If she could just prove to herself that heights weren't so bad, she could book a plane ticket home for her dad's birthday in February.

But that wasn't looking likely now, even with Arden here to hold her hand.

"Well, I'm going up," Arden finally said. "It's a clear night."

Incredulous, Rosie gasped. "You're going to leave me here on the stairs?"

"You're more than welcome to join me." Arden shrugged, brows lifting expectantly.

"Arden…" Rosie bit her winter-chapped bottom lip so hard that she tasted blood. She couldn't do this. Every fibre in her body was screaming that she couldn't. Her heart was crushing itself between her ribs. Her stomach was cramping and twisting and writhing. Even if she didn't fall, she might very well shit herself, and that would be just as terrible and traumatising. Especially in front of her new girlfriend who she hadn't even dared break wind in front of yet.

Arden softened, stepping back down to Rosie's level. Her voice was echoey in the empty stairwell. "You're brave enough to do this, Rosie. I know you are. The only person you have to prove this to is yourself. You did the zip line, remember?"

"Yes, while sobbing uncontrollably."

"You still did it."

"This is different." Rosie eyed the stairs in front of her, and they seemed to watch her, too. Waiting.

"This is easier. You won't be swinging from a harness. Your feet will be firmly on the ground. It's just a few more steps and then a lot of standing around."

Arden made it sound so simple. Rosie wished it was. Still, Arden was right. She wasn't risking certain death this time. She wouldn't be dangling from a wire in the middle of the woods. She would be on top of a building, with solid concrete beneath her feet and railings protecting her from the edge. So what was holding her back?

Maybe she just wasn't brave enough.

She was about to admit defeat when Arden's honey-soft voice stopped her. It was the same one she used in the shower in the mornings, melodic and timid and a little bit shaky, but it always reminded Rosie of mermaids somehow.

And she was singing Rosie's favourite song; the song that made her feel brave and capable. The song she'd sung on the tree's platform. "Rocket Man."

Rosie couldn't help but smirk, a surprised chuff falling from her when Arden's voice rose on the chorus. She was in her happy place, with a person who had once been a stranger in a window and yet now knew exactly how to help her. And she did only have one level left to climb.

She let Arden pull her up, and they hummed

the lyrics together as they conquered the steps. And then they reached the door, an icy draught kissing them hello as it opened. Rosie didn't stop singing, and she didn't pause. If she did, she would change her mind, and she didn't want to back out now. She was here. She was brave. She was a rocket man about to brave the skies.

Arden tugged her forward, into the night. It was quiet, with only a few other groups leaning against the railings, some of them snapping pictures on expensive cameras fixed to tripods, and others chatting as though they weren't three hundred metres above the rest of the city. If they could do it, so could Rosie.

"I'm a rocket man," she repeated, squeezing her eyes shut against the harsh wind.

"Open your eyes, Rosie." Arden was still leading her forward, closer to the edge, further from her comfort zone. But there was still the sturdy floor holding her up, and there was nowhere she could fall save for the places she already had with Arden.

So she did.

A gasp caught in her throat as speckles of silver and gold light flooded her vision. It was like standing above the stars. Like she was on the moon, looking over an entire galaxy, only this one wasn't an empty vacuum, though it was boundless. It was New York. Her home now. She'd felt like one of the ants on the street when she'd first moved here: unimportant and tiny. Now she was tall, and she wasn't alone because Arden was holding her hand. Now, she'd found what she'd been searching for.

And that knowledge, that feeling, that certainty, was so strong that she didn't think about all the ways she could fall, or all the ways she wasn't supported. She didn't think about the height at all. She was here. She'd made it.

"It's so beautiful."

Arden nodded proudly, her gaze still fixed on Rosie as though it could anchor her. "It is. And you made it."

"I did."

"Not so bad, is it?"

Rosie shook her head, too awestruck to say much more.

"Good. Because you're getting on a plane to Manchester in two weeks to see your family."

She snapped back to attention again, her eyes glossy both from the cold wind and the view. "What? Pardon?"

"I already bought the ticket." Arden's blonde hair whipped across her face, and her attempt to scrape it back was in vain. "You're homesick, Rosie, and that's okay. You needed to prove to yourself that you could get back on a plane, and now you have."

"But... you didn't have to..." Rosie stuttered, her chest burning. "I could have bought the tickets."

"But you wouldn't have. You would have put

it off until it was too late because it's scary and you don't think you're ready. But you are. Look at you. You're ready."

It was true. Rosie wouldn't have been able to find enough bravery to book a flight yet. Now, she didn't have a choice — and she could do it. She would. Tears rolled down her cheeks as she pulled Arden into a tight embrace, where everything felt easy and right and wonderful and she wasn't afraid of falling because she already had. "Thank you. Thank you so much, Arden."

"Of course," Arden whispered. "As long as you're not gone for too long. You better come back."

"Of course I will. New York is home now." *You're home now.* It was too soon to say it, but it felt like the truth.

Triumphant, Rosie dared take the final step to the railings. Her stomach swooped, but as long as she gripped onto the railing and Arden's hand, she was fine. At the edge of their little universe, the Hudson wended beneath the Brooklyn Bridge, and below her, the Flat Iron wedged itself between a fork in the road. It was beautiful and it was home, and Rosie no longer doubted it.

Especially not when she caught a billboard flickering on one of the tower blocks.

"Oh my God, that's my face." She pointed to the advertisement for Don't Be a Stranger. When Caroline had dubbed Rosie the new face of the brand, she'd meant it very literally. Now Rosie didn't just work behind the scenes to market the app. She told her story for magazine articles and wrote her own blog posts to share with users: tips for dating in New York, red flags, how to know when someone was right, and so on... She signed them all as she did her posts on the app: Love, Rosie. Everybody knew her real name now, just as she knew many of the people she'd met at the mixer personally. It was taking off, and Rosie had quite a social media following so that people could keep up with her love story.

It hadn't been why she'd come here, but Rosie loved it. She was passionate about connections and romance, and working hands-on for Don't Be a Stranger meant she could follow that passion and help others too.

She had lots to come home to, then, after her trip to Manchester. Lots of things she couldn't leave behind. The most important one, the reason she had found so much, stood in front of her now.

"Don't forget me when you're famous," Arden teased, slipping her fingers between Rosie's.

Rosie rolled her eyes and leaned into Arden's warmth, her breath visible in the night air. "I thought they'd use a better photograph. I look like I'm about to sneeze in that one."

"Shut up. You look perfect. You always do. Shall we go and get coffee?"

Rosie deliberated this. Something tugged her to stay here. She wanted to savour this moment, on top of the world. "Nah. Let's stay a bit longer."

So they did, and Rosie let her fears wash over her with the moonlight. Arden held her close, her arms wrapped around Rosie's waist, and her chin resting on Rosie's shoulder. And they stayed and talked and loved, and Rosie no longer felt as though she was searching for anything at all.

She'd found everything she'd needed. She'd found more than she'd ever thought possible. She'd found Arden.

About the Author

Bryony Rosehurst is a British romance author dedicated to telling diverse stories of love and happily ever afters — and perhaps a little bit of angst sprinkled in for good measure. You can usually find her painting (badly), photographing new cities (occasionally), or wishing for autumn (always). Chat with her on Twitter: @BryonyRosehurst.

Manufactured by Amazon.ca
Bolton, ON